The Widow
of
Martin Black

Tales from the Macabre Imagination

of

David Lewis Paget

BARR BOOKS

Dedicated to my friend Keith A. Fowler
For his faith in me
and my work

Other Poetry available by the author:

Pen & Ink — The Complete Works 1968-2008
Timepieces — The Narrative Poetry
At Journey's End — The Narrative Poetry, Vol. II
The Demon Horse on the Carousel — and Other Gothic Delights
Poems of Myth & Scare
The Devil on the Tree — and Other Poems of Dysfunction
Tales from the Magi
Taking Root
The Storm and the Tall Ship Pier
The Book on the Topmost Shelf
Tall Tales for Tired Times
Butterflies
The Season of the Witch
Smugglers Pie
My China — Poetry in and about China
The Red Knight — Selected Poems

http://www.lulu.com/spotlight/david_lewis_paget

Introduction

Edgar Allan Poe is considered by many to be the premier writer of the macabre, both in story and in poetry. Yet it is my pleasure to introduce to you the man who continues where Poe left off. David Lewis Paget is an accomplished Australian Poet. His narrative poems are of such high quality both in rhyme and meter that there are few his equal. The characters in these narratives will capture your imagination, inspire your fears, and maybe even provoke a tear or two.

Over the past forty years or more, David Lewis Paget has honed his skill as a Narrative Poet to such a degree that his ability to scare and yet also touch the heart are as sharp as any knife. I became acquainted with David's writings only a year ago while searching for a good volume of poems to read during October, and was considering more of Edgar Allan Poe's work when a copy of "The Devil on the Tree & Other Poems of Dysfunction" appeared on the internet. I took a chance on this Poet, unknown to me at that time, and read it in one sitting, cover to cover, and found myself chilled to the bone. I then began my search for other volumes by this reincarnation of Poe, and found fifteen volumes of the same type of beautifully written narrative poetry that could either bring a tear to your eye, or freeze your heart with the utmost fear. Why listen to me? Don't! Read them for yourself, make yourself comfortable and read each one until you find there are no more, and yet find that you desire just one more, and one more.

I do have one suggestion, I would not read these poems alone, I would find a good friend to sit with and read them together. I would also check all closets, under the bed, and every dark attic or basement before reading. Oh, and turn on all the lights as well, or you can be brave and read them in the dark, but have a local hospital in mind when your fear becomes your partner, and Death comes a-calling.

Keith Fowler   July 2015

The Widow of Martin Black

Always a bit of a mystery,
She lived in a seaside shack,
Would go to town when the sun was down
The widow of Martin Black.
She always went in her mourning dress
And a veil that covered her face,
'Do you think she'd date,' I asked a mate,
'You wouldn't be in the race!'

'There's a list of suitors, long as your arm
Just waiting to take her out,
They knew her back on her Daddy's farm
When Martin wasn't about,
But he trumped them all with his shiny Porsche
With his black cravat and coat,
And in the bay not a mile away
With his V6 Jet-ski boat.'

'You tell me she was a good time girl
In love with material things?'
'She certainly liked the odd gemstone
And her hands were covered with rings.
But that was him, with his taste for gold
That he liked to shower on her,
And parade her down in the glitz of town
With bling, and covered in fur.'

'And yet, I've not seen a single chain
Or a necklace, brooch or ring,
She's so austere when I've noticed her
I've not seen anything,

She wears a drape of the blackest crepe
And a veil that hides her eyes,
But pauses there when I stop and stare
As if caught in some surprise.'

'That isn't much of a mystery
If you knew the couple, Jack,
You might as well be a twin of him
The fabled Martin Black.
She'd think that his ghost had risen up
If she saw you in the street,
You might just give her a heart attack
If your dress is not discreet.'

I went back home to the mirror, donned
A coat and a black cravat,
And topped it off with a load of bling
And an old black stove-pipe hat,
The type they said that he used to wear
When they roamed abroad at night,
Taking in all the music halls
To dance till the early light.

She saw me there in the street, and screamed
Then rushed at me and attacked,
And cried, 'you're not going to spoil my dreams,
You'll not be coming back!'
Her fists had pounded my solid form
Til she stopped, collapsed and cried,
And babbled out a confession that
For long, she'd kept inside.

The last I heard she was with the police
Who had questioned her all night,

Extracted all of the details of some
Long and drawn out fight,
They took her down to the waterfront
Where the Jet-ski boat was kept,
And then began to rip up the floor
As the widow wailed and wept.

And he was there with a livid scar
Where she'd slashed him in the throat,
Stuffed him under the planks and boards
By his pride and joy, the boat,
I didn't know he had disappeared
When I'd thought to bring him back,
But all I'd caused was a host of tears
For the Widow of Martin Black.

The Winding Path

I met myself on a winding path
With the beach ten yards away,
Walking slowly towards me then
By the pounding breakers spray,
The path was narrow, I stepped aside
As I felt a twinge of fear,
We both were startled, I heard us say,
'What are you doing here?'

I looked at me as I must have been
At the age of thirty-one,
And I was visibly shaken, seeing
Just how the years had gone,
'I'm not quite how I envisaged me,
Were the years ahead so hard?'

I felt a chill and replied to me,
'I was hoist on my own petard.'

'What has become of our hopes and dreams,
The ones that we must have shared?'
'I let them slip through my fingers, once
I noticed that no-one cared.'
'I always said that I'd have to fight
For the things that I held dear,'
'But the years have changed, and rearranged
For none of those things are here.'

With one last look at each other, we
Then parted and turned away,
I to a desperate future,
And me to my dying day,
The I then turned that was thirty-one
'Can you tell what happened to She?'
I couldn't remember the one I meant,
'She's certainly not with me!'

The Blood of an Englishman

There was always something strange about
The tree by the clifftop farm,
It hadn't been there when I was young
Till the storm blew down the barn,
Then once the land was cleared it grew
At a pace I'd never seen,
A raggedy, twisted wreck of a tree
That my wife said was obscene.

'Why don't we cut it down,' she said,
'Why do you let it grow?'
'It doesn't do any harm,' I said,
'It's there for the winter blow.
It stands where it will protect the house
From the fiercest winter storm,
It may be ugly to see,' I said
'But it helps to shelter our home.'

The roots were massive and twisted, and
They spread, all over the place,
They tunneled under the house and then
Came up by the fireplace,
I chopped them off and I poisoned those
That tried to come through the floor,
And then I found there were other roots
Jamming our old front door.

The winter came in a rush that year
And we were buried in snow,
We hoped that there'd be an early thaw
But it didn't hurry to go.

We stayed inside and we stoked the fire
With the roots I'd cut from the tree,
The food went down in the larder, but
The fire burned merrily.

I hadn't so much as glanced outside
For a month, or maybe more,
The wind would howl at the chimney pots
But to go outside, what for?
Then Spring shone over the windowsill
And the snow began to melt,
So finally we could venture out,
I can't tell how we felt.

For out there at the side of the house
The tree had grown grotesque,
It seems it had continued to grow
Beneath its snow-clad vest,
For branches snaked across to the roof
And clung to the chimney pots,
To hold itself upright and aloof
Where I'd chopped the roots right off.

But what had disturbed and frightened me
Was the tree had grown in height,
Its gnarled and twisted trunk so high
It was almost out of sight,
It disappeared in a darkening cloud
That seemed to hover and stay,
While other clouds were adrift up there
It was still there, day by day.

At night, with terrible grinding sounds
The branches moved on the roof,

They tumbled off the chimney pots,
Believe me, that's the truth!
The wife said, 'We should have cut it down
When we had the chance, last Spring,
But now it'll probably take the house
So we can't do anything.'

I know you'll never believe me now,
It all seems so absurd,
But I broke out the elephant gun
At the sound of just one word,
We lay abed with it overhead
And the tree began to hum,
It woke me as I listened, and then
The word I heard was, 'Fum!'

I aimed the gun up the tree that night
At those penetrating sounds,
I couldn't have fired enough if I
Had had a thousand rounds.
And something hurtled on past me then
To land right down in the bay,
The tree was silent, it ceased to hum
And I chopped it down next day.

Purple Doom!

I'd not seen them out in the open,
They grew in the alleys and lanes,
A purple flower with a sort of power
In the scent from its pores and veins,
I asked Romana the name of it
But she shuddered and turned away,
'It's a type of bloom called Purple Doom,
Or that's what the gypsies say.'

The scent was sickly and sweet out there
I admit, it went to my head,
Romana came to the caravan
And made crazy love in bed.
The scent was an aphrodisiac
That drove normal men insane,
Our clothes were dropped and we couldn't stop
Till we cried aloud in pain.

The aftermath was a migraine head
That we both endured that night,
And when we woke, she tried to choke me,
All we could do was fight.
At last when we came back down to earth
And surveyed the shattered room,
Romana said that we could be dead
From the scent of that Purple Doom.

I beat the weeds round the caravan,
I poked and prodded and pried,
Found Purple Doom, there in the gloom
So its scent was sweet inside.

I tore the clump right out by the roots
But I cut my hand, it bled,
I burnt the flower, curtailed its power
But with poison in my head.

I don't remember the next few days
But I almost passed away,
I seemed to be wandering in the dark
Where the sky was always grey,
A castle rose in a fallow field
And I tried to cross the moat,
I called Romana 'Lady Gay'
And she said, 'Just stay afloat!'

But flowers assailed on every side
They were purple, pink and red,
Leaning in with their tendrils, seemed
To sip the blood I bled.
A gypsy shook me awake one day
And I slowly came around,
'Don't go bringing your caravan
And camping on gypsy ground!'

He'd gripped Romana by the hair
And tried to drag her away,
But she let loose with a gypsy curse
And he turned and fled that day.
We towed the caravan away
And avoid all lanes and gloom,
But she retains a potpourri to
Make love with that Purple Doom.

The Script

From the time that Alison woke she knew
That she had to speak her lines,
It was part of some strange assignment that
Had lodged, deep in her mind,
And every day had begun like this
From as far back as the Prom,
For every day was a part to play
Though she didn't know where from.

Her lines appeared in her deepest sleep,
Were as glue upon her page,
She wasn't allowed to deviate
Protest, or express her rage,
She'd go to Milady's ballroom all
Dressed up with bustle and flare,
Plastered with ancient make-up and
A Pompadour in her hair.

And Alan, down off the ballroom he
Would finish his last cigar,
Straighten his wig and tails and take
His boots on into the bar,
A tumbler there of Cognac he'd
Toss back, then head for the ball,
Looking to share his heart out there
With the fairest one of them all.

He'd met her before on other nights,
She'd hidden behind her fan,
Her lashes were long and fluttered then
As he tried to hold her hand,

But she had proved to be skittish, she
Would lead him along, then stay,
And disappear in the dancers there
As she struggled to get away.

But Alan was more determined now,
He pinned her against the wall,
Caught the scent of her heaving breath,
'Don't you care for me, at all?'
She'd hesitate as those hated lines
Once more came into her head,
'Oh my, this maiden is blushing, sir,
My cheeks are burning red.'

He led her towards an ante-room
For a long desired embrace,
But he couldn't see behind the fan
The anguish on her face,
She wanted to live and love, she thought
She wanted to cry aloud,
But all that her script would let her do
Was gravitate to the crowd.

And Alan was so frustrated,
He thought that he'd never score,
For Alison seemed to disappear
As he opened the bedroom door,
And she stood out in the coffee room
With amazement on her face,
Where had he gone, she'd closed her eyes
To wait for his sweet embrace?

Alan tore off his tie and wig
And he hurled them to the floor,

Why did she always disappear
Just there, at the bedroom door?
He flung about, and he just went out
With his face so set and pale,
'I'll not be staying a moment more
In a Barbara Cartland tale.'

He had wondered where his speech came from
It had seemed so stiff and trite,
Embedded into his head, it seemed
When he was asleep at night,
He jumped on into a cab outside
In a vain attempt to flee,
When Alison ran beside him then
And cried, 'Hey, wait for me!'

No Escape!

'I'm coming to get you now,' he said,
'I'm coming to get you tonight!'
Derek sat with his headset on,
His face was white with fright.
'I think you have the wrong guy,' he said,
'It couldn't be me you mean!'
'Oh yes, I'm coming to get you now,
I know you, Derek McLean.'

He sat there silent as eerie chills
Spread up and along his spine,
A face came on his computer screen
That rang some bell in his mind.

'This better not be a joke,' he said,
'You'd better not mess with me!'
The voice in the headset chuckled low
In some evil deviltry.

'It's taken a while to track you down,
But track you down I did,
You should have stayed off the Internet,
Covered your head, and hid.'
'I've nothing to hide from,' Derek said,
But his voice broke high in alarm,
'You'll never be able to block it out,
That day on Emerson's Farm.'

At the very mention of Emerson's Farm
The listener held his breath,
For years he'd struggled to block it out,
The site of that childhood death.
They'd played together in sodden fields
And had ventured into the marsh,
Thinking to pick the bluebells there
But the end of that was harsh.

'I'd like to know who you are,' he said,
But his words came out in a whine,
'You know full well, do I have to tell,
I'm here for the second time.
You left me there and you ran on home
As I sank in there to my neck,
You had no care for my tiny life
But tonight, I'll teach you respect.'

Derek shuddered and hit the switch
To turn the computer off,

But nothing flickered, the screen stayed on
And Derek began to cough.
'Have you any idea what it's like to drown
In a sludge of grass and mud?
It isn't pleasant, I'll tell you that
You should try it once, you should!'

Derek coughed and began to choke
In a fit of remorse, and fear,
He'd tried to forget the little bloke
Who had haunted him, year by year.
The doctor, when he examined him
Said, 'Heart attack, and he choked.
His eyes are staring, as if in fear
And there's mud in the back of his throat!'

The Amulet

'I am so tired, so tired,' he said,
'So tired but cannot sleep,'
He lay there restless in his bed
But could not even weep.
'I'm all wept out,' he would have said
If she'd been there to hear,
But he lay in an empty bed
Since she had disappeared.

'It's not as if she left a note
To say she'd not be there,'
He watched the light bulb spider weave
A web above his stare,

She'd gone down to the market at
The other end of town,
And though he searched, she'd left his world
She'd turned it upside down.

The stallkeepers had seen her there
She'd gone from stall to stall,
Whenever she'd go shopping she
Would want to see it all,
Her endless curiosity
Had kept him home that day,
His legs would never carry him
The miles she'd walk that way.

'Go try the stall that sells the scarves,
I'm sure I saw her there,'
She never did do things by halves
Of that he was aware,
'Go see the stall with rings and things,
She bought an amulet,
A silver chain, all old and stained
And placed it round her neck.'

He'd looked in vain to find the stall
For he had packed and gone,
'We didn't really want him here
With such a carry-on,
He dealt in spells and tiny bells
And readings in his tent,
We wondered what was going on
Then he packed up, and went.'

And no-one saw which way he'd gone,
They didn't even try,

'We didn't want to mess with him,
He had the evil eye.
Two other guys have lost their wives
As well, since he came here,
They go into that tent of his
Then seem to disappear.'

'He kept a cage of spiders, that I know,
I saw them there,
Of many different colours, weaving
Cobwebs in the air,
He said they were his weavers, making
Gossamer, so sad,
He'd sell it in the Faery Dell, he said,
The man was mad!'

'I am so tired, so tired,' he said,
'So tired but cannot sleep,'
He lay there restless in his bed
But could not even weep.
He watched the light bulb spider weave
A web above his stare,
And cried aloud, 'Where are you, Eve?
I'm lost in my despair!'

Marooned - (a dual ending)

There was mist up high on the mountain
There were bones along the shore,
And a line of caves that met the waves
Around that evil tor,
There were screeches in the forest
But they weren't from parakeets,
And the heavy sound of breathing
Late at night, and from the deeps.

While the waters round this island
Seemed to mutter from the reef,
When the tide would urge them forward
They would pile and then retreat,
It was if it was forbidden
For the waves to beat the shore
As an ancient Atavism
Gave out its primal roar.

So we camped out there on the beaches
Within sight of Hartley's wreck,
That the reef had torn a hole in,
There was water to the deck,
It sat forlorn on a sandbar
Within reach, when the tide was low,
We hadn't a plank so the vessel sank
And we had nowhere to go.

We lived on fish that we netted,
We traced out 'Help' on the sand,
We hoped that a plane from overhead
Would rescue our little band,

There was John who was the bosun,
There was Jane who cooked and chored,
Myself for the navigation,
And Hartley, that made four.

But seven others were lost at sea
Were afloat beyond the reef,
The tiger sharks had left their marks
With their cruel razor teeth,
So we kept a silent vigil
With the single flare we had,
And hoped that Keith would bring relief
In the merchant 'Iron Clad'.

(for alternative ending, jump to *)

'We need to go in the forest,'
Said Jane in a bleak despair,
'We need to find what fruit and berries
Might just be growing there.'
So John went off with a bucket
As the sun began to rise,
But soon was back, he had been attacked
And was missing both his eyes.

'A thing rose up in the forest,
It had no shape or form,
It just looked black but it still attacked
And I felt my face was torn,
It had a gutteral growl as old
As the earth that formed this place,
A sense of aeons before the storm
That created the human race.'

He died that night with a whimper,
With everyone else asleep,
I began to shake as this evil shape
Was taking him up the beach,
It dragged him into the forest,
Food for its larder there,
And I so scared and unprepared
That I fired our only flare.

It lit the heavens above us,
It lit up the sand, and then
It lit the trees in the forest
And the bones of other men,
When Hartley woke with a curse and spoke
The most welcoming words he had,
As Jane got up from her sleep, he cried,
'By God, there's the 'Iron Clad!'

(Alternate ending from *)

When Hartley woke in the morning
We saw he had gone quite mad,
For John lay dead with a bleeding head
And a wound where he'd been stabbed,
While Jane took off and ran up the beach
To shelter in one of the caves,
And I was forced to listen to him
Engaged in one of his raves.

He was blaming John for wrecking the ship
And blaming me for the tack,
'You were the Navigator, Jim,
So what do you say to that?'

I said that the fog was thick and deep
When we drove up onto the reef,
'And you should have been up on the deck
Not down in a drunken sleep!'

He went for me with the rusty blade
He'd used already on John,
But I was younger and far too quick
As he came stumbling on,
I wrestled him to the ground and found
The knife had entered his side,
Then belching blood on the sand he cursed,
Lay on the beach, and died.

When I went to look for Jane I heard
A single scream in the cave,
Where a giant octopus held her,
I was just too late to save,
It's tentacles were ten feet long
And were wrapped around her frame,
Though I slashed and cut off three of them
She was dead before I came.

So I wandered back to the lonely beach,
The only one alive,
My heart so low at this latest show
That I thought of suicide,
But then out there in my bleak despair
I fired the flare we had,
And there, beyond the reef I saw
The shape of the 'Iron Clad'.

The Magic Pen

He was nothing if not successful,
Grant Overman with his pen,
Everything that he seemed to write
Was well received back then,
The publishers fought for his stories,
And women swooned at his tales,
The only negative feeling then
Was coming from jealous males.

Was coming from jealous writers,
Who never quite got it right,
Their work returned from the publishers
To give it a 'second sight.'
'I don't see how he can churn them out
So fast, with never a flaw,'
Said Ernest Benn to his leaky pen
While blotting his tale once more.

'I think he's in league with the devil,
He's scribbled a pact in blood,
Or how could he twist my heartstrings so,
My tears come in a flood.'
His wife had sniffled through seven books
Of the hated Overman,
But never wailed at her husband's tales,
He'd not yet published one.

'I have to discover his secret,
There's something we just don't know,
If only you can get close to him
To see how his stories flow.

He needs a helper to clean his house,
Apply for the job, and then,
Rummage around what can be found
And watch him, using his pen.'

She used her charm at the interview
And was taken on to sweep,
To wash the dishes and scour the pans
To clean, three days a week,
While Grant would sit in his study there
And sit, bowed over his desk,
Then fall asleep in his padded chair
While he thought of tales burlesque.

Marie came back on the second day
And she said, 'I think I know,
The thing he's got and that you have not
That makes his stories flow.
He keeps it locked in a bureau drawer
Till he starts to write, and then,
It dances over the page, I swear,
He slept through chapter ten!'

'You say the pen does the writing?
I see,' said Ernest Benn,
His eyes aglow, 'so at last we know,
He has a Magic Pen!
We need to get it away from him
So that I can find success,
The chances of getting caught are slim
If we do this with finesse.'

Marie left open the kitchen door
On an afternoon in June,

While Ernest, unobtrusively
Sneaked in, and hid in the gloom.
Though Grant was falling asleep, his hand
Had begun to race again,
So Ernest battered him from behind
While Marie took hold of the pen.

But Grant sat up, and he tried to rise,
He cried a hollow note,
Marie hung onto the pen, and then
She stabbed him in the throat,
And blood was suddenly everywhere
The desk, the floor, their shoes,
Said Ernest, 'better get out of here
Before we make the News!'

After he'd washed and filled the pen
With a nice new brand of ink.
He held it over the paper, said
'Do I even have to think?'
The pen began on its sudden scrawl
But was making quite a mess
By writing a line in blood, not ink,
'I, Ernest Benn, confess!'

The Final Muse

'I think I've come to the end of things,'
He said, without a tear,
'But I don't mind, for I cannot find
A reason to be here.
The hopes I cherished are in the past,
The dreams all come undone,
I look ahead to the future and
I know, there isn't one.'

He sat alone on the patio
And stared on out to the bay,
'There was a time,' he began again,
Then stopped in his dismay,
For whitecaps out in the ocean still
Were rolling in to the shore,
Just like they had on another day,
Just like they'd done before.

And pictures came to his aging eye
Of the world, how it had been,
When life and love were a world away
When he was just sixteen,
But times and tides had rolled over him
In a restless, reckless ride,
Had torn the very heart out of him
To leave empty space inside.

'There must be a time,' he thought aloud
'When it's right to call it quits,
When you've done the things that you wanted to
And it's fallen all to bits,

With friends and lovers gone on their way
And with not a glance aside,
While I, stiff-necked, and so correct,
Am caught in the sin of pride.'

And then, the thought of his darling wife
Had finally raised a tear,
The sense he'd not even noticed her
For the time that she was here,
'We never know what we've got,' he thought,
'Til it's well and truly lost,
Just one more line in the ledger that
Adds up to the final cost.'

Then the children, what of the children with
That look of innocent trust,
Who burrowed into that heart you had
When you thought that God was just,
But once they're grown and you find they've flown
To their lives, to stand or fall,
You wait for them to return to you
But you find they never call.

'I think I've come to the end of things,'
He said, without a tear,
'But I don't mind, for I cannot find
A reason to be here.'
The only sound was the breaking waves
With the salt-spray and its sting,
He looked about like a man who craves,
But none were listening!

The Last Kiss

'I always wanted to see your face,' she said,
She was teasing me,
I'd gone along to our twentieth wake
Since we'd been divorced, and free.
We got on better than ever we had
When chained together in time,
That piece of paper had choked us both
But being apart, sublime!

I looked across at the massive cake
They had wheeled across the floor,
'Now that's what I call a giant bake,'
I said. She said, 'There's more!'
There were twenty candles around the top
And seven around the lip,
The twenty since we had been divorced
And seven for when we flipped.

The seven year itch was what it was
When we ended up in court,
We really should have got over it
But we'd given it little thought,
For the plumber lasted a month or two
She confessed, in one of her gripes,
For she got bored with him on the floor
Checking her taps and pipes.

And I got sick of the Dolly Bird
Who had lisped, she would be mine,
Who liked to strip to the Beatles hits
When her head was full of wine,

It all fell flat when the passion died
And we stopped to get our breath,
There was nothing she had to say inside
So she bored me half to death.

We came together just once a year
As a mark of our mistake,
And every year with the slightest tear
We would share a Parting Cake.
I'd never seen one as big as this
It was white, and frilled with lace,
And that's when Jennifer said to me,
'I wanted to see your face!'

The lid flipped up and the stripper rose
As I dropped my jaw, and gaped,
She stood a moment and struck a pose,
'That's my present for you, Jake!
It's a bit too late to apologise
For making that awful scene,
But I think we're older now, and wise,
And you get to lick off the cream!'

The girl was covered in cream all right
On her thighs and hips and breast,
'You get to lick what you want tonight
And I'll scrape off the rest.'
She laughed, I laughed, and I saw her then
As the face of one I'd missed,
There was little thought of the stripper then
As we both leaned in, and kissed.

Tongue-Tied

He watched as she passed each morning,
Same time, each day of the week,
But his lips were dry and his tongue was tied
And he found he couldn't speak.
She had such a heavenly beauty,
That he'd raised her up on high,
So how could he, a poor mortal seek
Such a goddess, up in the sky?

Her hair the colour of ripened corn
Her lips the pink of the rose,
The dimple sitting in either cheek
And the tilt at the end of her nose.
Her eyes would flash as she passed him
In that wonderful glide and sway,
He almost spoke, but he always choked,
And cursed as she walked away.

While she kept steadily walking,
She never would look around,
Though the sight of the young Adonis made
Her heart pit-patter and pound.
He looked like a Grecian statue,
From the Pantheon of the Gods,
Why would he spare a glance at her
With her features all at odds?

For the blonde was out of a bottle,
And her eyes, they must have looked scared,
She tried to appear so nonchalant
And not that she really cared.

But she walked that way each morning
Just to get a glimpse of him,
Hoping he'd say one word to her
That would be encouraging.

The days passed on through the Summer
Then Autumn had come to stay,
And he still stood each morning
And she still walked that way,
But he paced in desperation,
Chewed his fingers down to the bone,
'When would he pluck the courage up,'
She thought, as she passed his home.

They seemed to be making progress,
For they'd nod as she walked by,
But he didn't see as she raised her eyes
Frustrated, up at the sky,
She'd put on a brighter lipstick,
Mascara, as black as coal,
While he despaired as she disappeared
At the emptiness in his soul.

He practised before the mirror,
And tried out a 'How are you?'
But shook his head at the words he said,
It simply wouldn't do!
What if he came straight out and cried
The thoughts he felt in his heart,
'I've fallen so much in love with you
That it's tearing me apart!'

While she broke down in the ladies room
The moment she got to work,

Her friends came gathering round to say,
'He must be a total jerk!'
But she flared back to defend him,
'I think that he fancies me,
He stands and nods like a Grecian God
But his face is misery!'

The morning came that he steeled himself
And walked right into her path,
While she stood still as she broke a heel
And sat with him on the grass.
'You can't go to work like that,' he said,
'My name, by the way, is Bill.'
'I often wondered,' she smiled at him,
'And mine, by the way, is Jill.'

Hothead!

They said he was always a hothead,
As a kid he'd scream and shout,
He got so bad, made his mother mad
That his father locked him out.
He couldn't get in at the windows,
So wandered all night round the farm,
And by the time that his folks were fine
The kid had set fire to the barn.

On the day he got out of Borstal
He was just turned seventeen,
And the Warder James said, 'Listen Ames,
Better keep your fingers clean!

There isn't a future in anger,
And less of a future in crime,
So keep your head, though your hair is red
Or you'll be back, doing time!'

But any advice flew over his head
And headed on out to the stars,
For soon young Ames was making his name
Hanging in clubs and bars.
He never went home to his parents
For which they would say, 'Thank God!
He got his genes from his Grandma Steenes,
And she was distinctly odd!'

He had a passion for fire, would sit
For hours, and stare at the flames,
They said his eyes would be hypnotised
When playing his thermal games.
He'd light a match in a pile of thatch,
In a wood or a field of gorse,
Then watch the firemen put it out,
Well hidden away, of course.

They wouldn't take him as a fireman,
They said he was up to his tricks
When they saw him next to the fire house
Lighting up piles of sticks,
Then Sheriff Bruce said he had no use
For a hothead in his town,
And put the word on the street; he heard
They were going to hunt him down.

So he hid in the Church's belfry,
And up in the Town Hall clock,

Then sit and fume in that tiny room
Til he finally ran amok,
He broke in just about midnight
According to Fireman Tuck,
Who'd come from his farm, and raised the alarm
'He's stolen the Fire Truck!'

Then fires broke out in the woodlands,
And fires sprang up in the town,
While the chief said, 'Look for a big red truck,
It must be somewhere around.'
They called out the local constabulary,
They called out the National Guard,
And orders came from the top to say,
'Go out, and hit him hard!'

They cornered Ames in a one-way street
Where he couldn't turn it around,
So he climbed on up to the top of the truck
And they finally gunned him down.
The coroner ordered an autopsy
On the body of Hothead Ames,
As the circular saw dropped his skull to the floor,
His brain burst into flames!

The Fall of the Earl of Grace

One last night in the dungeon,
One last night to his fall,
The Earl of Grace was chained in place
To the damp of the dungeon wall.
They'd taken him at the tourney,
The knights of the Duke of Beck,
While the King had turned his face away
As they fettered him by the neck.

They'd taken his chain of office,
They'd taken his rings and seal,
The shifting tides of the time had sighed
In showing him what was real,
The King had removed his favour,
The court had looked on askance,
That final fall from a height so high
Was part of the courtly dance.

For no-one survived forever,
In that court of grim intrigue,
He'd been aligned with the prince to find
The prince was brought to his knees.
Grace didn't have the King's permit
To marry the Lady Grey,
And that, just one of the sins he wore
Conspired to put him away.

For Beck was stalking the lady,
The wealth and the lands she had,
Her cold response to his needs and wants
Had driven the Duke quite mad.

The prince, confined to his quarters
Was backing the Earl of Grace,
But once the marriage had come to light
The scandal had brought disgrace.

He stood in the dark, and shivered,
In the hour before the dawn,
And watched them setting the gallows up
That would take his quaking form.
Beck had wanted the axe and block
But the King had murmured, 'No!'
'I'll not part him from his noble head,
But I'll hang him, long and slow!'

The hangman came at the dawning,
Was strapping his hands and feet,
While shuffling him to the drop, he said,
'Hanging an Earl's a treat!'
And Beck was there to await him,
To whisper his evil spite,
'You'll be deep in the earth, while I
Will be with your wife tonight.'

They took their time with the halter,
Were seeming to draw it out,
When down in the court a clatter,
Of knights, and an awful shout:
'The King is dead, long live the King,'
As they rescued the Earl of Grace,
Shuffled him off the drop, and then
They hung the Duke in his place.

Jonathon Brown

'I'm looking for Nathan Cory,
I'm looking for Jonathon Brown,'
That was the woman's story,
In a pub, this side of town.
I'd only gone for a quiet pint
And hoped to be on my own,
Til this angry face burst into the place
And I put my beer mug down.

'Would I be my brother's keeper,
To follow him near and far?
He may appear, but he's never here,
You can try the public bar.
Jonathon flits from place to place,
You never can tie him down,
I should know, I'm his brother Joe,
At your service, Joseph Brown.'

She ordered a double Vodka,
With a twist of lemon, squeezed,
Then sat on the stool beside me,
Without a 'you mind?' or 'please'.
'And what of this Nathan Cory,'
She said, 'Is that just a friend?'
And I thought back to the nursery,
With that dark wall at the end.

'Oh Nathan, yes, well he comes and goes,
He isn't a friend to me,
But Jonathon always speaks of him,
Has known him since he was three.

He's not a guy you should tangle with,
He's always wanting to fight,
Jonathon used to go with him
When he came to him at night.'

'You say you've never seen Nathan, then,
Not once, in all of your days?'
'I try to avoid the ones that cause
Me strife, in so many ways.
My brother and I, we live apart,
I haven't seen him for years,
That Nathan came in between us two,
A bit like the family curse!'

Her smile was gentle, her eyes were brown
Her hair fell over her face,
She didn't seem quite so angry now
But I saw she carried Mace.
The men in white came up to the bar
As I dashed my beer down,
They said, 'Hello! Whoever you are,'
And I said, 'I'm Jonathon Brown.'

The Blank Page

This page is white as a white can be
Til I lift my pen and trace
A scrawl of black from an inky sac,
A tale of the human race.
I pick and choose, who wins, who lose
Their brief duet with fate,
Who twist and turn as they live and learn
To dance at my garden gate.

I paint in the cliffs and the sky above,
The shingle, down on the shore,
A tiny cottage that's full of love
With a garden of herbs, and more,
A man who walks on the winding path,
He's a difficult man to gauge,
Will he be happy, or sad, or what
When I get to the end of the page?

I'll call him Clive, for he's so alive
When he gets to the cottage gate,
His eyes are bright in the fading light
As he looks for his darling, Kate.
She hears the creak of the hinges greet
The one who captured her heart,
And races out through the cottage door,
Who am I, to keep them apart?

But the world is cruel and there's always gruel
To add to a perfect tale,
I should be telling this up at the pub,
Over a pint of ale.

But I'd have to muddy my story up
To make my listeners tense,
And what does it take but a big brown snake
To add to the tale's suspense.

The snake came slithering out of the herbs
And reared it's head up high,
I could be mean with the following scene
As the snake bites Kate in the thigh.
But I'm only here to fill the page
Not to lay a bloody trail,
So Clive, alive to the danger leaps
To seize the snake by the tail.

Our hero takes the snake by the tail
And cracks it like a whip,
Shatters its spinal cord and so,
That was the end of it.
There's a smiling face and a swift embrace
And a tale untold, for sure,
When Clive and Kate shut the creaky gate
And enter the cottage door.

I only wanted to tell a tale
To banish this page of white,
The page that mocks like a sly old fox
When I stare at it each night.
So take the story of Clive and Kate
Who live on top of the cliff,
And dream sweet dreams if your own life seems
Too bland, and think, 'What if?'

The Note

'It's not that I wanted to leave,' he wrote,
On a scrap they later found,
'Just that the stress was too intense,
You drove me into the ground.
You're like a terrier, won't let go
Til you drive us all to tears,
You have to worry the same old thing
You've clung to your chest for years.'

'It's not as if you can let things go
When you've lashed, and whipped and scourged,
You won't let the pain just go away
Though I've pleaded, and I've urged.
I've read the letters you wrote before
And it's word for word the same,
You said you were writing your demons out
But I see that nothing's changed.'

'When will you learn that a man's a man
With his rights and wrongs intact,
You can't go changing a leopard's spots
With your mouth, and that's a fact,
You share your misery every day
Til it's all far too intense,
You think your way is the only way
And allow no recompense.'

'Why did I ever stick with you?'
I ask of the stars above,
'The answer comes, as it does with you,
'I stayed for the sake of love!'

What is this love but a trail of pain
From a scar that will never heal,
That rakes the ashes, over again
Til our love can't see or feel.'

'It's not that I wanted to leave,' he wrote,
'But it's better for you and I,
There must be someone better for you
And I'll put my faith in the sky.'
He'd dipped his pen for the final time
As despair had come in a flood,
And she had muttered, 'I don't know why,'
That he'd signed his name in blood.

The Many Lyves of....

I'd never felt comfortable in that house
Not once, since we'd moved on in,
A rambling, derelict, barn of a house,
Three storeys of age-old sin.
Nobody said there'd been murders there,
Or told of the gypsy's curse,
Three hundred years of discarded junk
And I don't know which was worse.

The air was dank, and creepy and cold
So I opened the windows wide,
Trying to get some airflow through
To clear the smell inside.
It was musty, dusty, smelt like a tomb
With a corpse, decayed and grey,
We cleaned and scrubbed it room by room
And the smell went slowly away.

We tackled the ground floor first, we thought
We could leave upstairs til last,
The stairs were blocked with a French chaise longue
From some distant time in the past,
It was jammed hard up by the bannister rails
So it wouldn't go up or down,
I said I'd have to pull it apart
And that sparked a Hartley frown.

Hartley was the love of my life
Who tackled that house as well,
She said it was a pig in a poke
That its real name was 'Hell!'
But we finally cleared a space to live
And she worked out a way to shift
That French chaise longue from the stairway by
Trying a twist and lift.

The second floor was a nice surprise
There was none of the junk and grime,
The bedrooms still remained as they'd been
Laid out in another time,
So Hartley dealt with the dust in there
While I went up for a look,
The room above was an attic room
And that's where I saw the book.

It lay on a dusty table with
Its pages ragged and torn,
The paper a sort of parchment and
The ink, quite faded and brown.
The cover was ancient leather, cracked
And worn, as if by an age,

'The Many Lyves of this House' it had
Embossed, as a title page.

I cautiously opened the cover, read
The words on the parchment page,
The light in the room then turned to gloom
And a storm began to rage.
I raced on down to the ground to find
A man outside, who said,
'For those inside, don't seek to hide,
I say, bring out your dead!'

And a cart stood out in the street outside
A pile of the dead in place,
The street was cobbled, not like before,
But of bitumen, no trace.
And on my door was a huge red cross
With a white and painted scrawl,
'God, have mercy on us,' it read,
'Have mercy on us all.'

And there on the floor, inside the door
Was a corpse wrapped in a sheet,
I dragged it out by the feet, no doubt,
And I left it in the street.
On climbing back to the topmost floor
I leapt and pounced on the book,
But the page had turned, and the fire burned
Before I had time to look.

London burned in the distance and
Lit up the night like day,
I didn't know of it then, but it
Was burning the plague away,

And every page in that cursèd book
Brought a different time to bear,
'The Many Lyves' that this house had lived
Were all inscribed in there.

I slammed that leather cover shut
And I laid it on its face,
Then swore that I'd never open it
While the Lord would lend me grace.
And Hartley, dragged from her cleaning chores
She never could understand,
Why I put a torch to that ancient house
And burnt it to the ground.

The Breakdown

'I don't remember a year like this,'
She stood by the window pane,
Staring into the murk and mist,
'All that it does is rain!
It's barely stopped for a month or more
And the garden's all a-flood,
The line is down and the washing's drowned
And the yard is thick with mud.'

I'd just come down from the nearest town
On the other side of the hill,
'Strange, it hasn't been raining there
And the sun is shining still.
The mist is clear, just a mile away
And the hedgerow's full of life,
I came to see if you'd heard or seen
A glimpse of my darling wife?

She looked confused for a moment there
Then she shook her head, real slow,
'I don't recall if I've even seen her
Since she got up to go,
She said she needed to find herself
The girl that she used to be,
Before she married and settled down,
Well, that's what she said to me.'

'You don't think she's had a change of heart,
A tiny hint of regret?
I thought by now she'd have worked it out,
And wouldn't be so upset.'
'I doubt if she will be coming back,
She said it wouldn't be soon,'
I turned away and my face was grey
On that painful afternoon.

She stood up close to the window-sill
And all she could see was rain,
Despite the fact that the sun shone still
And the skies were clear again,
The nurse came in and she said, 'It's time,
We must get your wife to bed.'
And I drove over the hill in pain
Just wishing that I was dead!

A Long, Long Way from Home

My father lies in an orchard,
My mother lies at his side,
But once, a million years ago
He made that girl his bride.
And love was all that they knew back then
In that world of endless time,
They conjured me in a magic glen
And they shared their lives with mine.

But life is merely a dripping tap
With a leak that can't be sealed,
And much as we'd like to take it back
Once lived, it can't be healed.
It drips away through our laughter,
It drips away through our pain,
It slips away on our sunny days
And fills our gutters with rain.

We've seen where that grand horizon lies,
So far away for the young,
And seek to fill it with needs, and deeds
That never will be undone.
But while we're chasing our dreams and schemes
Ignoring what we were told,
That life is merely a race to run
The people we love grow old.

And one by one they depart from us
Like a breath of wind in the trees,
With nothing to mark their passing now
But a stone in the cemetery.

The end of time comes to all of us
When that tap will cease its drip,
That dreaded death that will take your breath,
Your mind, and the rest of it.

And people say it's a void that takes
Our memories, one by one,
My folk live on, though a long time gone
In the mind of this orphan son.
I sometimes sit, and I think of it
On the grey of their granite stone,
And weep for the years they've been asleep,
I'm a long, long way from home!

Maidenhair

The grave they kept on the lonely beach
Lay under a foot of lime,
Most of the pile had washed away
With rain, and the tides of time,
It had been so long since its stone was laid
As a warning to who went there,
The rough-cut name had begun to fade,
To the solitary word, 'Despair!'

It said, 'Despair if you dig it up,
Despair if you set it free,
It savaged the girl called Maidenhair
It ravaged this fair country,
It roamed the farms at the dead of night
And tore into sheep and hogs,
The farmers called it the devil's blight
When they found their blood-spattered dogs.

The only monk that was left to tend
The grave, now lay in the church,
His Order gone, now the only one
To fend off the tidal surge.
The church was almost a ruin since
It had shattered the oak-backed doors,
And blasted the Brothers altar with
Its devils breath, and its claws.

But the monk lay ill, and he knew full well
He never could make the beach,
To pile the lime on the Beast of Time
And the sea would surely breach.
His fellow monks were all laid in clay
On the upper side of the cliff,
Their duty done, they had one by one
Passed on, and lay cold and stiff.

A crack appeared in the bed of lime
With a rush of air from the shore,
And something groaned with an eerie moan,
The seed of the devil's spore.
A whisp rose out of the open grave
To join with a gully breeze,
That sent it whirling along a wave
And into a grove of trees.

And then an ominous rumble rose
As a whirlwind formed on high,
It whipped the waves to a surly peak
As it rose to blacken the sky,
A tempest, such as had never been
Tore trees, like beeches and birch,

And cut a swathe like the path it paved,
On its wayward way to the church.

The monk lay there with his gilded cross
As he heard the beast outside,
It gave a roar by the shattered door
And the monk had almost died.
But a gentle hand took the cross from him,
A hand that was soft and fair,
And held it up to the beast so grim,
The ghost of Maidenhair.

It shuddered once as she stood with ease
And the cross then drove it back,
The whirlwind died to a gully breeze
As it fled back down the track.
It seemed confused, and it seemed to lose
Its overwhelming reach,
And sank back into its limestone grave
On that long deserted beach.

The sea had battered the arching cliff
Hung over that limestone shore,
It now collapsed in a final lapse
With the monks who'd passed before.
And beneath a thousand tons of earth
That is holding off the sea,
There's a rough-cut stone that says, 'Despair,
Despair if you set it free!'

The Black Box

The truck pulled up at the crack of dawn
On a Sunday morn in June,
I could hear the men unloading from
The darkness of my room,
'What a strange time to deliver,' I thought,
As I rose, pulled on my socks,
For there on the porch outside I found
They'd left a big black box.

There wasn't a mark on this gleaming box
But the scrawl of my own address,
Nothing to say who it was from
Just a silent emptiness,
I left it there til the sun came up
Then I pulled it through the door,
And there in a tiny script was writ
The legend, 'from Zhongguo'. *

Why would the Chinese send a box,
I hadn't been there for years,
Maybe the Tong I'd tangled with
Back then, for black was a curse.
I looked for a way to open it
But there wasn't a flap or seam,
It wasn't tin and it wasn't steel
But a substance in-between.

I dragged it out in the garden then,
Outside of the door, at back,
And thought that I would figure it out,
Then the box began to crack.

It heated up in the morning sun
And began to peel away,
Opening up the inside to
Be seen by the light of day.

And there inside was a giant egg,
The biggest I'd ever seen,
All sorts of curious markings on
The shell, in Mandarin.
I went inside and I locked the door
And I sat myself to think,
Why would they send a giant egg?
My mind was on the blink!

It only took a couple of hours
In the sun, that day in June,
And the shell began to break apart,
To hatch in the afternoon,
And a thing crawled out of that empty shell
That I never thought I'd see,
A tiny Chinese Dragon hatched
Came out, was suddenly free!

I couldn't believe how fast it grew
As it fluttered out its wings,
It ate the cat and my bowler hat
And a host of other things,
Then it wandered down to the goldfish pool
Slid in, and began to swim,
There isn't a single goldfish left
And the pool is sizzling.

Its head comes up and it gives a roar
And it sets the reeds on fire,

The flame is almost ten feet long
And my future's looking dire.
Will someone get in touch with the zoo
They can have the beast for free,
Oh no! It's wandering up the path,
No doubt, it's looking for me!

*Zhongguo – pron. Jong gwar – China

The Cave

A single bullet was all it took
And I needn't have wasted that,
He sat alone in that dismal cave
In an old Field Marshall's hat,
His eyes were sunk in that pallid face
A demented cast to his jaw,
He didn't move as I knelt and aimed
And put an end to the war.

It was getting late, it was '68
When I ventured into the cave,
My friends said going spelunking was
A bit like digging your grave.
'Expect big rats, and giant bats,'
They said, before I'd begun,
So I added that to my haversack,
Just to be sure, a gun.

It wasn't a normal cave I sought
But one by the autobahn,
Where I'd seen a crevice opening up
That nobody else had done,

It seemed to lead deep down in the earth
Could easily close, if found,
So I took a pick, a dynamite stick
And burrowed into the ground.

I had a lamp on my helmet, like
A miner's, casting a beam,
And climbed on plenty of rubble
That had collapsed in a steady seam,
It led to a concrete tunnel
Plenty of rock strewn passageways,
A giant work of construction that
Lay hidden in former days.

I seemed to go on forever
Then ran into a barbed wire cone,
Blocking one of the passageways
And a sign, 'Halt! No Go Zone!'
The wire was rusty and fell apart
As I pushed it away to the side,
But then the sound of scuffling rats
Brought the gun out by my side.

Then finally it had opened up
Into what would appear a cave,
With flags and banners arranged about,
The glory of former days,
A corpse sat propped in an easy chair
In a uniform from then,
And there, attached to the shirt front was
A nameplate, 'Bormann, M.'

Beyond, and under the banners was
A barely human form,

Who stared at me in the darkness there
As if I'd not been born,
The greatest conqueror of our time
And there's no disputing that,
Lost in pain in his vast domain
For there *der Führer* sat.

If Ghosts Could Lie

He stood at the end of the pier that day
In hopes that they'd ask him on,
But Marilyn had just sailed away
With his elder brother, John.
He stood and scoured the horizon till
The sun went down in the west,
Then turned and wended his way back home
Though he'd get but little rest.

He tossed and turned for an hour or so
But he couldn't get to sleep,
Then crept on out of his bed, he thought
He might take a little peep,
For out of his bedroom window there
The sea shone under the Moon,
The surface calm as a millpond as
He fell back into his room.

And his dreams that night were turbid dreams,
Obscured like a murky pond,
Where he couldn't see the half of it
Viewed through the slough of despond,
Had he lost the only love he had,
And the brother he loved so well?

59

The morning dawned on a sudden storm,
And the sea, with a giant swell.

There wasn't a sail on the sea that day,
There wasn't a boat at all,
The yacht was found all smashed around
The end of the stone sea wall.
They said there wasn't a soul aboard
Whoever there'd been was gone,
He didn't know who he mourned the most,
His Marilyn, or his John.

John came to him in his sleep that night
With his eyes all brimming with tears,
'I shouldn't have taken her out, despite
I'd loved the woman for years.
But don't blame her, it was only me,
For she made it plain that day,
She'd only come for a friendly sail,
And then she pushed me away.'

And Marilyn came to his dream as well
With the seaweed caught in her hair,
'I shouldn't have gone with your brother John,
Now I'm lost beyond despair.
He said you'd come, but he sailed away,
Said, 'just a bit of fun,'
But now I weep in the ocean's deep,
It's the end for everyone.'

They found the bodies beyond the pier,
They were floating, hand in hand,
And when they got them ashore they found
That she wore John's wedding band.

They never appeared in his dreams again
And he thought it just as well,
If ghosts could lie, he at least could cry
As he wished them both in hell.

The Coffin Bell

He lived in a fine old country house
Befitting a man of means,
With everything a Victorian Squire
Could aspire to, in his dreams.
He owned four-fifths of a colliery
In the days when coal was gold,
And topped that up with a Brewery,
But the mean old man was cold.

For Benjamin John Fortescue ruled
His house like a would-be Earl,
His son had never felt welcome there
Since he'd married a country girl,
The mother had gone some years before
Who protected, in his youth,
But now, the butt of his father's whims
The lad found out the truth.

He treated them like the servant class
Expected to fetch and bring,
But paid a pittance to keep them there,
His purse on a miser's string,
'I keep a fine roof over your heads
And you eat each day for free,'
He'd say, whenever they asked for gilt,
'What more do you want from me?'

Their toddler Tim wore cast-off clothes
And was made to play outside,
'I don't want a ragamuffin's mess,'
He'd say, till the mother cried.
'You don't seem to love your grandson,' said
His son, his head in a whirl,
'I would if he had some parentage,
But not from some country girl.'

As time went on there was something wrong
For the father suffered fits,
At first it would start with a seizure,
He would seem to lose his wits.
He'd lie for days in a sort of haze
And would scarcely draw a breath,
And Caroline would look hard it him,
'It's as if he's caught in death!'

It happened enough to make him plan
Should the doctor be deceived,
'I don't want the fools to bury me
Alive, so I'm not retrieved.'
He bought a coffin with space inside
And a tube, out to the air,
With a little bell he could ring as well
If he found himself in there.

'Be sure to follow instructions if
You think that I am dead,
Affix the bell to the tube as well
With a cord down to my head,
Then check the grave for a week or more
To see if the bell should ring,

Then hurry to dig me up, and I
Will give you anything.'

The day came that on the seventh fit
They could swear that he was dead,
'There isn't even a breath of air
And his eyes are up in his head.'
Three doctors came, and they all concurred
That his life was now extinct,
'It had to happen,' the couple heard,
'He's been living on the brink.'

They laid him out in his coffin, and
They fitted the tube to breathe,
Attached the bell, and the cord as well
Before they rose to leave,
But Timothy stayed to play that day
As he did, down in the Dell,
And a week went by till his mother cried:
'Where did he get that bell?'

The Man Who Lived in the Cave

We'd moved on in to a clifftop house
When our babe was very young,
I had to erect a barbed wire fence
To keep our darling at home,
For Ellen was a precocious child
With a beautiful, smiling face,
But for all our efforts to tame her down
It was hard to keep her in place.

She would bounce about, would run on out
The moment we turned our backs,
Many a time I would see her climb
And she'd give us heart attacks.
'She's halfway up the chimney, John,
She's climbed right up to the thatch,'
The wife would cry, and I'd almost die
In bringing our daughter back.

She'd stand awhile by the cottage gate
That led on out to the track,
That wound its way right down to the bay
On a narrow, winding path,
I wired the gate, and I thought it held
Till the day she broke on through,
And made her little way to the bay
Before we even knew.

I found her at the mouth of a cave
That sat just up from the shore,
And breathed a sigh of relief as we
Embraced, like never before,
But she pointed in to the darkened cave
With her tiny little hand,
'I want to go in the cave with him,
That funny old sailor man!'

'There isn't a man in the cave,' I said,
'You must have been seeing things.'
'Oh no! He asked me to follow him
And he showed me lots of rings.
He had a black patch over his eye,
And a ponytail in his hair,
I want to go where the sailor goes,
Will you let me go in there?'

I carried her back up the winding path
Though she clung to me and cried,
'That cave is simply an eerie place
And it's cold and damp inside.'
I should have taken more notice then,
I thought it was just a rave,
For days, young Ellen would speak of him,
The man who lived in the cave.

I went to check at the library,
The history of the town,
And read that smugglers used that cave
When nobody was around,
And long before there were buildings there
A smuggler on the run,
Had sheltered there in that dismal cave
With his daughter, Ellen Gunn.

I raced on home to the clifftop house
To find young Ellen gone,
The wife was having hysterics there
And I was overcome.
I ran, pell mell down the clifftop path
It was such a deathly scare,
And searched to the end of that awful cave
And I found her Teddy Bear.

A fisherman on the beach had seen
Young Ellen on the sand,
Then watched as a sailor took her in
To the cave there, hand in hand.
'I thought that he was her father,' said
The rustic fisherman,

'She seemed quite happy to go with him
And he looked a kindly man.'

I must have searched it a dozen times
And I called, and cursed, and cried,
And prayed to god that I'd find my girl
Hid somewhere deep inside,
When out of the depths, she toddled out
Stood still, turned back to the cave,
And that's when I glimpsed that sailor man,
Who stood at the back, and waved.

The Spawn of War

He met his Dad for the first time when
His father came marching home,
After the war to end all wars
From London through to Rome.
He'd never seen him before he stooped
As if to pluck out a thorn,
And asked his Ma in his army suit,
'Just when was the young one born?'

He hadn't been home for five long years
And Jeremy then was four,
He constantly seemed to be adding up
The years that he'd been at war,
His Ma would say, 'He's a miracle,
Young Jeremy went full term,
I carried him for a year,' she said,
'It must have been wartime sperm!'

Then his father growled, and his mother howled
As he placed her on his knee,
And running his hand on sacred ground
Said, 'all this belongs to me!'
His mother cried when he said she lied
In the years of his growing up,
And treated him, apart from the rest
When he called him a 'scoundrel's pup.'

His father clung to his Khaki suit
It was washed and pressed each week,
'You never know when they'll call me up
If this treaty doesn't keep.'
He worked back down in the coal mines where
He'd emerged to answer the call,
Black from coal like a demon's soul
But he'd gone, to fight for them all.

But Jeremy never saw him smile,
He never could do enough,
The others would go on trips the while
But Jeremy got a cuff,
'What have I done,' he'd often say
As his father sat and yawned,
'Don't come bothering me today,'
And mutter of 'wartime spawn.'

The years went on and the son had gone
To live on his own, nearby,
But always came to visit his folks
Each month, till the one July
He came around to the house and found
That the dust his father choked,
Was sat so deep in his lungs that he
Had suffered a massive stroke.

'Your father's down in the hospital,
He might not ever come out,'
His mother cried, while his brother, Clyde,
'He's all washed up,' he'd shout.
The others wouldn't go visit him
They had much too much to do,
So Jeremy took his favourite book
To visit him in Ward 2.

His father sat in a wheelchair there
And he looked up in surprise,
'Nobody's come to see me, lad,'
He said, with tears in his eyes.
'Why, of all people, would you come,'
As he helped him into his cot,
'What do you think, you silly old man,
You're the only Dad I've got!'

And he read to him from his favourite book
And he sat and held his hand,
And the years of hurt that disconcert
Lay buried in No Man's Land,
For the feeling came back in his limbs
As the father did atone,
And Jeremy came, the spawn of war,
'Come on, I'm taking you home!'

The Perfect Circle

'Time is a perfect circle
Where it ends, it curves back in,
Starting a whole new cycle
Where the other one begins,
We cannot escape our futures, nor
Much less, escape our past,
The things that we've run away from
Will be waiting there, at last.'

That's what he said to Jennifer
As she packed her final case,
And carried it out to the taxi,
'I don't want to leave a trace!
I'm parcelling up the memories
That I shared so long with you,
And dropping them off at the station,
Locked forever, on platform two.'

And Derek had looked forsaken as
She passed out through the door,
She'd said their love was mistaken
It had gone, forevermore.
'Don't look, enquire, or ask for me
Or you'll still be waiting yet,
The one thing that will stay with me
Is that I wish we'd never met.'

And so she passed on out of his life
A marriage of thirteen years,
A time of strife with a testy wife
And a basketful of tears,

He tried to cling to the better times
That were fading in his head,
He only knew that he loved her still,
Though he wished that he was dead.

When Jennifer rode away that day
She had thought, 'At last, I'm free!
I'm going to live my life the way
That I hoped my life would be.'
She thought of her husband's final words
As his heart began to rend,
'Just know that I love you, Jennifer,
I'll be with you in the end.'

She moved to a whole new neighborhood
And she spurned her former friends,
Went with a whole new clique of folk
Who had never made amends,
There wasn't a single married pair,
They were all divorced, or spent,
Adrift in the dim-lit bars like her
In search of what life meant.

But when the news of his passing came
She was pensive for a while,
She planned to go to his funeral
And forgot for a day to smile,
He hadn't been able to countenance
A life where his love had gone,
And left a note with a single quote,
'I'd best be moving on!'

She drifted on for a few more years
In her false, gay party hat,

With nobody there to wipe her tears
As he'd done, when times were flat,
When time brought on some dread disease
And she knew that her time was spent,
Whose hand would pay for her funeral,
Not one, and nobody went.

They had to open her husband's grave
That he'd paid in the years before,
When life for him had been content
'Til death do us part,' he swore,
And as her coffin was laid on his
In that dismal outback track,
It was then I heard but a whispered word,
'I knew you'd be coming back!'

The Lord of Judgement

The lamplighter held his pole up high
And rapped on each window pane,
'Fix your shutters and pull your blinds,
Prepare for the coming rain.'
His footsteps sharp on the cobblestones
Held everybody in dread,
'Snuff the candle and say your prayers,
Tomorrow you may be dead!'

And the gaslamps gave a flickering glow
In the empty streets and lanes,
While the Moon shone pale through the trees below
Lighting each window pane.
'Prepare to pay for your darkest sin,
Reflect on the deeds you've done,

71

Sit round the table and, holding hands,
Wait til the storm has come!'

Then a wind blew cold through the narrow streets,
With the sharp, cold sting of rain,
And in the distance the lightning flared
Where the Lord of Judgement came,
And nobody dared to breathe a word
That the monster might come in,
With breath of fire and a flashing sword
In his search for Carolyn.

But she sat deep in a dim-lit room
And she held the town in thrall,
Since ever her love in a dismal tomb
Was found, and she blamed them all.
She ringed the town with a purple mist,
They couldn't get out or in,
And wailed out loud in a mourner's shroud,
'You'll pay for this deadly sin!'

Then Carolyn sat by an empty hearth
And arranged a pile of bones,
The skull of somebody once she knew
And a pair of magic stones.
She placed the stones in the socket eyes
And the jaw began to move,
'If only you'd loved as he loved you,
But your brother disapproved.'

She sat herself by the oracle
And listened to what he'd say,
She crossed herself with a hazel twig
And the skull looked old and grey.

'Your brother took him aside one night
As a friend, and said, I quote:
'It's sad, so sad, but it has to be,'
Then he turned and cut his throat.'

So Carolyn sought her brother out
As he roamed abroad that night,
'I'm told you murdered my lover, Drew,
Can it be, can that be right?'
'I only did it to save yourself,
His love would have torn you apart.'
Then Carolyn moaned a dreadful moan,
And stabbed him, deep in the heart.

The lightning flashed and the sky lit up
Til it seemed as bright as day,
And the purple mist she had conjured, this
Thinned out, and drifted away.
You'll see her wander the silent streets
In a shroud, as if she's lame,
Her tears still running in lines and streaks
Since the Lord of Judgement came.

The Recluse

He hadn't lived in the world of men
Since he'd tossed his job, and quit,
He'd told his boss, 'There's no future here
And so, here's an end of it!'
The grimy city was getting him down
And the noise was driving him spare,
So he said goodbye to the world of fumes
To head for the open air.

He found a tumbledown cottage that
Nobody seemed to own,
The roof was keeping the weather out
So he thought to call it home.
He cobbled together some furniture,
A bench and a rustic chair,
And sat in the shade of the eucalypts,
And bagged the occasional hare.

The cottage was back off an ancient track
Unsealed, and long out of use,
The nearest cottage a mile away
In a similar state of abuse,
The pioneers had been and gone
Leaving just these standing stones,
A testament to a rugged life,
They were now just piles of bones.

Though at first the silence suited him
It would give him time to think,
He would lie at night awake and cite
That the sky was made of ink,
An ink shot through with pinpricks so
That the stars came shining through,
And feel, as the Autumn dampness fell
On his face as morning dew.

But Autumn shivered to Winter and
It would rain and pour for days,
He'd look on out to the distance where
All he could see was haze,
He'd keep a fire in the ancient hearth
With wood, when it wasn't wet,

And curse himself for short-sightedness
When it was, or he'd forget.

Then his hearing tuned to the many sounds
That he'd missed before in the bush,
The slightest sound of a twig that cracked
Or a breath of wind, at a push,
He heard the echo of silences
That whispered over the plains,
A spirit stirred that he'd never heard
Before, in his city pains.

But someone back in the world he'd known
Was worried that he had died,
And found the tumbledown cottage where
His friend was lying inside.
He wouldn't answer his queries when
He spoke in a human voice,
Such sounds were strange to a mind that ranged
When given a different choice.

Then the doctors came to check on him
And the police turned up en masse,
They said, 'We're having to take him in,
He'll harm himself at the last.'
But he raised one hand when they closed on him
In a manner distinctly odd,
And whispered 'Hush! If you strain you just
Might hear the voice of God!'

The Devil's Gate

I didn't see anything strange that day
When I first drove into the town,
If anything it was normal, though
I was breaking virgin ground.
I'd never been into this countryside
Before, with its mounds and mines,
A patchwork town with its mullock heaps
And its sad, neglected grime.

But the people there, they would stand and stare
As I drove my motor through,
They'd stop and stand on the corners there
With nothing better to do.
The mines had closed when the ore ran out
Though most of the miners stayed,
They didn't seem glad to see me drive
Or wave on their Grand Parade.

But I thought I'd stay in their tiny town
I was bushed, too tired to drive,
So parked the car by their only pub
And I ventured deep inside.
A man came out with a surly look
And he said, 'You're passing through?
I hope you're not a believer, son,
Or this town will do for you!'

I shook my head at the things he said,
I only wanted to sleep,
His questions rattled around my head,
But then seemed far too deep.

I paid for a room and locked the door
Then went to sleep for a spell,
But then discovered a woman there
By the name of Jezebel.

'Please help to smuggle me out of here,'
She said, 'in the back of your car.'
She whispered this with her ruby lips
Too close to my own, by far.
'Why don't you just get up and leave,
And walk right out of the town?'
'Nobody gets to leave this place,
If you try, he'll cut you down.'

I said that she wasn't making sense,
She was just confusing my head,
How could I concentrate, when she
Was sprawling over my bed?
'They thought they'd taken his power away
When they tied him up in chain,
But he only waits at his evil gate
For his thousand years of pain.'

'This town is under an evil spell
Since the miners found the rift,
If I said that my name was Jezebel
Then I think you'd get my drift.
He needs someone who believes in him
With a kind and gentle heart,
And that will help him to break his chains
Then he'll tear this town apart.'

I asked her where I could see the man
And she said she'd take me there,

But only if I could promise her
Not to believe, or care.
'He'll use his wiles, and his gracious smiles
To get at the heart that's true,
You have to reject, be circumspect,
Or he'll take the soul from you.'

That night I followed her down a mine
That was cold, and dark and damp,
The only light we could use that night
Was a feeble miners lamp,
But then we came to a giant rift
In that ground, of ash and slate,
And there was a dark and evil glint
From a wrought iron double gate.

A man was chained to that evil gate
On the other side of sin,
Unless we opened that Devil's Gate
There was no way he'd get in.
I stood surprised, for I saw his eyes
That were wise, before his fall,
'Have you brought me a true believer, Jez?'
For a moment, he stood tall.

'I brought you a non-believer, who
Will help me away from you,
I've wasted time on your promises,
For nothing you said was true.'
'Alas for me, will I never be
Set free to challenge The One?'
'No-one believes in the Devil now
So your power is all undone!'

There's a town that's tame, it has a name
But I'll not be telling you,
I don't want to see a believer there
To give the Devil his due.
For the fires that we all feared have gone
Since we learned we're not to hate,
It would only take one bended knee
To open the Devil's Gate.

The Starlings have to be Fed!

He'd go to the Square each afternoon
And sit on a bench, near me,
The one that stood in the shaded gloom
Of a brooding maple tree,
He'd roll his brolly and doff his hat
And scatter his bits of bread,
Then when the Keeper would tut, he'd say,
'The Starlings have to be fed!'

He'd watch them come in a darkening cloud
And scare the sparrows away,
Then sit and listen to what had risen
At this loose end of the day.
He'd sit and nod, and he'd take it in
As if he could understand,
This Starling patter that passed as chatter
Concerning the world of man.

I never once saw him take a note
Or even record the sound,
He didn't acknowledge the presence there
Of anyone else around,

He totally focussed on what they'd say
And cock his ear to their cries,
Then nod and smile in the strangest way
And shake his head at their lies.

Then after dark he would walk the park
And head for the studio,
That one dim lamp on the outer wall
Would show him the way to go,
And once inside you would hear him slide
On up to the microphone,
Where he'd tell his tales of success and fails
In a drawn-out monotone.

But you never felt a part of the tale
You were always shut outside,
Peering in from a ledge or bin
With a window open wide,
Then sometimes you were looking down
On the action from on high,
It could be from the bough of a tree
Or a wing in the azure sky.

He must have muttered a thousand tales
Of brooding, joy and despair,
The type of roles that would feed the souls
Of the folk who listened there.
They were light as vim, they were dark and grim
They were sown like seeds in the night,
And at the end, a beating of wings
As a bevy of birds took flight.

He entertains through the winter months
With a new tale every eve,

But stops as soon as the Spring comes in,
As the Starlings begin to leave.
They all return to their northern climes
With their tales to their Viking den,
While he will wait on the same park bench
For the winter to come again.

Behind the Hedge

The rambling house was all run down,
Well, what you could even see of it,
It sat in extensive, weedy grounds
And a hawthorn hedge surrounded it.
The windows hadn't been cleaned for years
The door was weathered, and boarded in,
They said that a hermit lived in there
Well hidden away from a world of sin.

And Sally was more than curious
Each time that we wandered by that way,
'How could he live so close to us
And never be seen,' she'd often say.
'He must be lonely, or maybe mad,
I'd love to wander the rooms in there,'
But I said nothing, I thought it sad
And bad that Sally could even care.

'I heard that he had a woman once
Before, when the house was nice and neat,
She worked in the garden there for months
And the house was visible from the street.
But that was before the hedgerow grew
And something happened, she went inside,

And never came out, not that I knew,
The rumours spread that the woman died.'

The weeks went by, she became obsessed,
'What if she's been imprisoned there?
Didn't they ask, or go and check?'
'Nobody knew, or even cared!
It happened so many years ago
And the garden overgrew with weeds,
Nobody wanted to even know,
Or interfere with a stranger's deeds.'

Sally would stand by the broken gate
And peer on in at the jungle there,
'Whatever you think, it's far too late,
They'll think you're mad if you stand and stare.'
'Somebody has to show they care,
I'm going into that house one night,
I want to know if she's still in there
And so should you, if your head is right.'

I said I wouldn't become involved,
So she went off on her crazy scheme,
Into the dark she sauntered forth
While I was asleep, and lost in dream.
She wasn't there when I woke at dawn,
I searched the house and I went outside,
Took in the rambling house's form
Then knew she'd gone, and I almost died.

I battled my way in through the weeds
And got to the house, the door ajar,
I called out, 'Sally, just come on out,
I need you back, wherever you are.'

The house lay still as an ancient tomb,
The air was chill and the rooms were bare,
The dust was thick in the morning gloom
For nobody had been living there.

And Sally sat on a tiny mound
Out back, and near the wooded copse,
The grave I'd dug, with a stone surround
And covered with blue forget-me-nots.
'You shouldn't have come,' I shook my head,
'What's done was done, and it can't be changed,
She left for a share of my brother's bed,
I would that it could be rearranged.'

But Sally sat with an empty stare
And I knew that I'd lost her then for good,
She didn't know of that other mound
That my brother made in that tiny wood.
'So this is the end of love that's lost,'
She said, with the merest wave of her hand,
'I'll leave you alone to count the cost,'
Then leapt to her feet, and turned, and ran.

The Pearl

It was not a salubrious neighborhood
As the townsfolk there would tell,
But you often found a gem of a pearl
In an ugly oyster shell,
And Derek thought that he'd found his pearl
In those mean and dismal streets,
A girl by the name of Jennifer Searle
Who would make his life complete.

He'd met her at a charity ball
On a short term holiday,
From where she sat, at the end of the hall
She'd taken his breath away,
Her eyes were such a delicate blue
And they held him in their stare,
He was like her prize, and hypnotised
As he stumbled to her there.

And she bade him sit beside her then
And she let him hold her hand,
And she hushed him when he tried to say
What he didn't understand,
Her smile was brittle, her hand was cool
And her skin as white as snow,
Her form was frail, but he felt her nails
Dig in, as he rose to go.

And a woman came to claim her then
Who dismissed him out of hand,
They waited until he'd turned to go
In a way that was pre-planned,

The woman gave him a printed card
With the girl's address at home,
And scribbled there, 'you may call on me
Just once, if you come alone.'

So he walked the damp and dismal street
And his heart began to sing,
He knew one call would be enough,
He would give her everything,
He found her door in a portico
With its number shaped in lead,
And rapped the brass of the knocker there
With its atavistic head.

Then the door swung slowly open and
He was standing in the hall,
Following tamely where she led,
The woman he'd met at the ball,
Jennifer sat at a table and
She smiled as he wandered in,
He stood and stared at her wheelchair
And his look was questioning.

'You get but a single chance with me
That's all that I ever give,
I've seen the lies in a hundred eyes
So rather than lie, just leave.
My legs have been useless now for years
But I'm whole, and full of love,
If you'd like to take a chance with me
Speak now, for I've grieved enough.'

'I fell in love with your eyes,' he said
'From the other side of the hall,

I didn't know that you couldn't walk
And it doesn't matter at all.
I wanted to offer you everything
If you'll have me, well and good...'
Then Jennifer blinked back tears, as she
Reached out for him, and stood.

The Word

It's only a week since I raised my head
From the depths of my favourite book,
The final tale in my library
And my basic foundations shook.
It had been so long since the world went wrong
And I fled from the things I heard,
To hide my head with the living dead,
And lose myself in The Word.

For the printed word is a friend of mine
Its sentiments never change,
It's comforting when you read a rhyme
That no-one can rearrange.
No matter how many have read it once
The story will still suffice,
You know that the ending will be the same
When you come back to read it twice.

But the world outside, it seems had died
With its people all grown cold,
There was nothing left I could recognise
From the world that I'd left of old.
There wasn't a smile on a single face
Or a humorous moment left,

There seemed a general loss of grace
With everything so correct.

The money hangs from the tallest tree,
Too high for us all to climb,
This world is new, belongs to the few
It certainly isn't mine.
Another stabbing, another death
Is all that I read out here,
And populations take to the boats
As millions live in fear.

Small wonder then, I wander the streets
To look for a library,
In the search for a book I've never read
On the way that it used to be.
A former time when the world was mine
I'll find it, by hook or crook,
For distant smiles and a woman's wiles
I'll bury my head in a book.

The Black Freighter

I'd met Helga at the Seaman's Rest
Where I said that I'd be her mate,
Sailing her ancient Freighter for her
Down to the River Plate.
But then, I'd never set eyes on it
I was more concerned with her lips,
This Helga, who had bought the wreck
From the old graveyard of ships.

Then down at the dock, I saw it then
Coal fired, and full of rust,
And wondered if it could make it there
But she turned, and said, 'It must!'
She'd spent the coin from a bad divorce
From the head of a shipping line,
'I helped him to build that business up,
In truth, it ought to be mine!'

It was then that I saw the hatred there
Set deep in her flashing eyes,
'My husband said he was going broke,
It was just a pack of lies.
He's bought another great tanker since
That he calls *Madrid Maru*,
And sails it under a foreign flag
So there's nothing that I can do.'

We threw some paint on the freighter then
And piled the coal in a stack,
Painted the name as *Helga Jane*
But the only paint was black.

She hired some Lascars, stoking coal,
An engineer for the crew,
And loaded the hold with tractor tyres
And aircraft engines, too.

We left the port with a head of steam
And nosed our way from the dock,
The pistons rumbled beneath the deck
In their first reprieve, in shock.
'It's been a while, it will settle down,'
Said the engineer, old Sam,
So slowly, out to the open sea
We sailed from Amsterdam.

The stars were bright on that first full night
With Helga stood at the wheel,
Heading into the darkness there
As if she could see and feel.
The Freighter seemed to respond to her
At the slightest touch of her hand,
And I took over the wheel once we
Were out of sight of the land.

I'd thought she might have been lonely
Once we had been some days at sea,
And hoped she'd open her cabin door
But her door stayed closed to me.
She seemed to brood, in an evil mood
When she joined me at the wheel,
'I gave him years of my life,' she said,
'Then all that he does is steal!'

And even the freighter seemed to feel
The sense of her own despair,

It rose and fell with the ocean swell
And groaned as if steel could care.
In black of night, with a single light
There were sounds deep in its bowels,
The hull would shake as I lay awake,
And moan, like a demon's howls.

A storm blew up on the seventh day
And it tossed our craft about,
We turned it into the crashing waves
As we tried to ride it out,
But the rudder snapped from the rudder post
So we couldn't turn or steer,
And all this little black freighter gave
The crew was a sense of fear.

Then out of the mist of the driving rain
Came a hull she thought she knew,
And Helga screamed, and the freighter seemed
To know it, *Madrid Maru*,
The pistons started to race below
And the bow rose out of the swell,
Racing towards the starboard now
Like an arrow released from hell.

Though Helga clung to the useless wheel
To try to steer it away,
All the hatred she'd ever felt
Reposed in the ship that day.
We threw the lifeboat over the side
And the engineer jumped free,
I called to Helga, and she replied,
'It's fate! It's coming for me!'

One of the Lascars made the boat,
The others were down below,
We watched as the Freighter raced ahead
While the tanker was long, and slow.
It punched a hole in the tanker's side
And was rushed by the water in,
With Helga fighting the useless wheel,
I never saw her again.

It took an hour for the ships to sink
Still lodged together with force,
Even while drowning in the depths
They couldn't get a divorce.
I'll never forget that Freighter though,
It took on a woman's pain,
They lie as one, now their day is done
Since we christened her *Helga Jane*.

The Proposal

I paced the floor by the tavern door
In the hopes she'd come my way,
She didn't know that I'd still be there
For I hadn't said I'd stay,
We'd parted there on a bitter note
On a dark and moonless night,
I'd told her I wouldn't marry her,
But now, I thought, I might.

I'd filled my head with the pros and cons
And the pros had come up short,
I'd have to steady and settle down
And that was my major thought.

I'd been so free that it seemed to me
I'd be hoist on a single hook,
Why would I trade a library
For the sake of a single book?

But then I began to doubt myself
As her scent came wafting through,
That scent of fire with the name 'Desire'
That she'd said, 'I wore for you!'
I'd pressed my lips to her silken throat
And I'd felt my power surge,
As she lay back and surrendered to
Some overwhelming urge.

Where would I find her likes again,
I paced, and bit at my lip,
We'd courted then since I don't know when,
She'd said, 'we're joined at the hip.'
But then I'd panicked and almost ran
I could see my freedoms gone,
'If you don't ask me, there's them that will!'
Like a fool I said, 'So long!'

I knew that she'd seen Montgomery,
He'd eyed her off at the ball,
And set up a wager, he to me,
He'd be first to see her fall.
She'd left that night in a coach and four
With him riding close behind,
While I'd returned to the tavern then
And drank til my eyes were blind.

I heard he was going to propose that night
And the thought had made me sick,

I'd have to make a decision now
And I'd have to make it quick.
I saddled Sally, the old grey mare
And I whipped her out the yard,
For Cauter Hall was at Risdon Weir
And I'd have to ride it hard.

We caught the coach at the meadow rise
And we passed it on the fly,
They must have seen a demon rider
And horse against the sky,
My cloak flew out as the wind blew up
On the road at Walker's Flat,
And somewhere there in the cold night air
I lost my only hat.

We skirted the ground at Risdon Weir
And we splashed on through the Ford,
The lights of the mansion grew more clear
As we galloped to Cauter Hall,
Her hooves a-clatter on cobblestones
I leapt from the horse's back,
And beat on the ancient cedar door
In a frontal, forced attack.

Montgomery stood in the passage there
And he turned to her to shout,
I raced on in with a sense of sin,
With a punch, I laid him out.
Catherine came from an ante-room
And she said, 'How dare you do...'
But I went down on my knees to her,
'I'm here for marrying you!'

She seemed surprised, then her laughing eyes
She tried to hide with a fan,
'I knew that you'd come around one day
If you saw me play with a man.
I'll take you dear, but I'll make it clear
That my guest was never the one,
We never marry our cousins here…'
Then I knew that I'd been done!

The Devil's Yacht

The yacht swept up in the dunes had been
Abandoned the year before,
I came across it, quite by chance
Some miles away on the shore.
The bow was buried, the mast had gone
I climbed and I peered inside,
And there in the cabin, it seemed to me
That somebody must have died.

There were stains of blood on the cabin floor,
Stains of blood on the sink,
Handprint stains on a cupboard door,
I took me outside to think.
Without a body the boat felt right,
I needed somewhere to stay,
And this was cosy and out of sight,
As free as the livelong day.

I used seawater to clean it up,
I got the cupboard to shine,
Whoever had bled in there before
This cabin would do just fine.

I found some blankets under the bunk
To set up a makeshift bed,
I felt like a proud new owner there
And the feeling went to my head.

I caught some fish in the darkening light
And cooked it there on the beach,
The flames had flickered and showed the mark
As high as the tide could reach.
A breeze blew up and I crept inside
Protected from wind and rain,
And sat, and pondered a lazy pipe
In there, where a corpse had lain.

It must have been after the Moon went down
I first heard the woman's cries,
Up from the shore, through the cabin door,
'You're always telling me lies!'
The wind was howling about the dunes
And the waves beat loud on the shore,
And over it all, the woman's wail,
'We've been through all this before.'

Then something clambered up on the deck
A thing with an ominous tread,
The hairs stood up on the back of my neck
As the woman wailed, 'You're dead!'
The thing jumped down to the cabin floor
In a shapeless gown of black,
All I could see were two red eyes
As it moved on in to attack.

The blade of a knife flashed by my face,
It gleamed in the light of the stars,

I tried to cry, 'Whoever you think
I am, I'm not, I'm Lars!'
But the blade sank home in my shoulder then
And I reached for it in pain,
I cut my hand on its sharpened blade
As it tried to strike me again.

That shapeless thing had let out a shriek,
Had glared with its two red eyes,
'Why do you hide on the Devil's yacht
If you're not a part of his lies?'
I tried to answer but nothing came
The pain swept me like a wave,
And blood was seeping from cuts and wounds
I was trying in vain to stave.

The figure turned and it left the yacht,
I staggered up to the deck,
And watched as it entered the breaking waves,
A sight I try to forget.
There were stains of blood on the cabin floor,
Stains of blood on the sink,
Handprint stains on a cupboard door,
They were always mine, I think.

For the woman that I'd been hiding from
Had sworn with her final breath,
'I'll seek you out, wherever you've gone,
It won't be a peaceful death.
I shall loose the demons from the hell
That you gave me, ready or not.'
How could I know that they'd find me where
I'd hid, on the Devil's Yacht?

Cyclops

He wandered at night the streets that might
Be busy, during the day,
The empty squares and the thoroughfares
To search for a come-what-may,
He'd never appear in the light of day
And shrank at a distant shout,
His way was always a lonely way,
Watching the lights go out.

He'd always avoid the gaze of men
Who would stare at him, then die,
Nor would he seek a mirror then,
He was born with a single eye.
His mother took him away at birth
So his father wouldn't see,
That she had lain with a cyclops once
And then paid the penalty.

She had kept him locked in a cellar, till
He had grown too strong and bold,
He'd strained and torn at his chains until
His jail had failed to hold.
He couldn't leave in the daylight, for
He had only known the dark,
So left one night in the pale moonlight
And escaped across the park.

He'd roam at night when the stars were bright
For the food and drink he'd need,
Padding the cobbled pavements there
In search of a missing creed.

What was the purpose of his life,
Could he exist alone?
Was there a female Cyclops somewhere
Willing to take him home?

One winter's night when the time was right
And the streets were damp and drear,
He saw her walking a way ahead
And quaked in a sudden fear.
What if she turned and gazed on him
Drawn in by his single eye,
What if she died? He shook and sighed,
'If she does, then so will I.'

She heard his footsteps behind her then
So he said, 'you're walking late!'
And her reply was a thankful sigh,
'I can't find my garden gate.'
He took her arm and they walked along
As she tried describing it,
His heart was full, he could do no wrong
As she tapped with a long white stick.

The Tale that Couldn't be Told

He'd been tapping away at the keyboard
So he could get the ending straight,
A labour of love he'd called it
But it was dark, and getting late,
The villain had to be sorted out
By the heroine, called Cath,
He wanted it all to jell before
That final paragraph.

The Moon had risen outside and shone
In a strange and subdued light,
He should have finished before, so this
Was not a welcome sight.
He backspaced over a typo, then
He looked hard up at the screen,
But all that he'd typed was gibberish,
In a font he'd never seen.

It must have jumped to another font
Was the first thing that he thought,
So he scrolled back up, to see how much
Of his work had gone for nought.
The font looked vaguely Arabian
With a hint of Russian too,
Had taken all of his storyline
So he didn't know what to do.

He tried to highlight the paragraph
And switch to the font he'd used,
But when he read what the wording said
It had left him quite confused.

'You've stumbled in to a place of sin
Have opened an ancient page,
Locked down for over a thousand years
You've opened the world to rage.'

'Delete the whole of the manuscript,
Don't let it stick in your head,
The more you read you will feel a need
And will probably end up dead.
Delete the curse, and the final verse
And destroy your hard-drive too,
Be sure, if you wish to stay alive,
To do what I tell you to!'

He thought of the work that he'd put in
And the rebel within him stirred,
'Why should I wear some other's sin
When I only have your word?'
The screen grew misty, and Cath appeared,
The heroine of his tale,
'Take no notice of him, my dear,
I'll die if his will prevails.'

His villain pushed her out of the way
And snarled at him through the screen,
'Where do you think my evil comes from,
Not from some fictional scheme!
You drew me out of an ancient well
Of lies, of sin and deceit,
To clear me out of your sub-conscious
You'd better hit the delete!'

He heard the footsteps pound up the stairs
And beat on his garret door,

'You'd better not have my wife in there,
Or else, I've told you before!'
And Cath appeared for the final time
In the tale that wasn't complete,
His neighbour beat on the padlocked door
As he sighed, and hit the delete.

The Face in the Frosted Glass

The old man came in the wintertime,
The mist was cold and grey,
She thought he'd been in a distant time
But then he went away.
She only caught but a fleeting glimpse
Through the hedgerow to the street,
But felt a chill as the memory spilled
From her head down to her feet.

He wore a common fedora hat
And a houndstooth overcoat,
The collar was turned up high, so she
Saw neither cheek, nor throat,
But just for a moment, as he turned
And beneath the brim of his hat,
She caught a glimpse of his piercing eyes
And his eyes were dull, and black.

She told her brother about the man
And she tried to laugh it off,
She said it gave her a sudden fright
And she thought that he would scoff.
Her brother turned with a furrowed brow
And his face was white as sin,

'If ever he comes to your door, you know
You never must let him in.'

'What do you know about this man?'
She cried, in a sudden fit,
'I only mentioned his passing, so
That you'd scoff, make light of it!'
A chill ran down to her fingertips
And tightness grew at her throat,
'Be sure to lock all your windows
And the door, please draw the bolt.'

He stood there facing the window, and
He stared long out at the lawn,
No matter how much she pressed him, he
Was firm, would not be drawn.
'There's no point letting the nightmares in
That will make you feel aghast,
The man you've seen is a walking sin
That we left behind in the past.'

She'd always trusted her brother John
Who was older, solemn, grey,
He'd always tried to protect her from
What hurtful people say,
Their mother had died, with her a child
While he was just sixteen,
They'd moved away to the countryside,
Had avoided kith and kin.

But John was working away at night
So it left her on her own,
Huddling over the fireplace
In their quaint and rustic home.

The mist swirled over the window panes
When she saw the face peer in,
And tap at last on the frosted glass
As he called out, 'Carolyn!'

'Carolyn, won't you hear me now
I have such a tale to tell,'
She stared back into the dull black eyes
Of a soul who'd been through hell.
She shook her head and she bit her hand
And she waved the man away,
'I need to talk to you, Carolyn,
Please hear what I have to say.'

She edged on up to the window
And she whispered, 'Please to go!
You know that you have me terrified
But for what, I just don't know.'
'They put me away for twenty years,
In jail, for killing my wife,
That woman you called your Momma, girl,
They sent me down for life!'

Carolyn shrieked, and held her ears
From the face in the frosted pane,
And distant memories flooded back
From her childhood, once again,
She saw them dragging her father off
But they never brought him home,
And John had gone to the funeral
Of their mother, all alone.

'They said I poisoned your mother,' cried
The voice through the frosted glass,

'I swear, my girl, that it wasn't me
But your brother John, alas.
I turned my back when your brother poured
That powder into her tea…'
Then Carolyn sobbed, and choked, and said,
'Please God. No! That was me!'

Gone Fishing

He'd ventured out with his fishing gear
Before the breaking dawn,
Packed the bait in his four wheel drive
And backed it across the lawn,
He knew that he'd be the only one
At that time on the beach,
And maybe catch, with the early worm,
From the rocks along the breach.

He'd parked the Ranger, doused the lights
Before he looked to see,
The miles and miles of sand out there,
But no sign of the sea.
It must have been one of those funny tides
That receded out of sight,
There wasn't a billow or breaking crest
Though the sea was there last night.

He climbed back into the Ranger then
And drove, while it was firm,
Way, way out, where the winter spray
Would freeze the air, in turn,
He must have driven a mile or more
But the sea was out of sight,

There were only deepening rock pools that
Were uncovered, overnight.

He stopped and parked by a monster pool
In the hopes there'd be a catch,
Long and deep where the fish would keep
Till the tide came rolling back.
He tossed his line with a baited hook
And it sank into the depths,
Until a flurry of water caught
His eye, and snagged his nets.

And then there rose to the surface such
A sight he'd never seen,
A pale and struggling girl with eyes
Of blue, and hair of green,
He hauled her in with his net until
Her strength began to fail,
And then he noticed that from her waist
Was a silver, fishes tail.

'My god, you must be a mermaid,' he
Exclaimed, but more in shock,
And she lay still and she stared at him
From a seaweed ledge of rock,
She didn't struggle, she didn't fight
But she held her arms up high,
As he gently lifted the mermaid up
And he swore he heard her sigh.

That was more than a year ago
And the sea's back, as before,
But he is more of a stay-at-home
Won't go fishing anymore.

He sits and plays by his covered pool
So the contents can't be seen,
And frolics there with the tiny fish,
And all of their hair is green.

The Black Stone Tower

I'd walked back home by the clifftop path,
I'd only been gone an hour,
Rounding the point, it came into view
The sight of our Black Stone Tower.
Its ancient mystery suited me then
We'd picked it up for a song,
Nobody else had wanted it,
At the price, we couldn't go wrong.

They said that a king had built it there
Far back in the mists of time,
And soldiers climbed by the old stone stair,
But now, thank god, it was mine.
A roof to shelter my Evelyn,
Though we supped by candlelight,
And drew our water deep from a well,
Made love when the stars were bright.

But now a breeze blew up from the cliff,
Was chill, and ruffled my hair,
And something about the Black Stone Tower
Was strange, a sense of despair.
For weeds had grown where the weeds were not
When I'd left, an hour before,
And someone had painted a bright red cross
On the Baltic Pine of the door.

It was only when I had got close up
That I saw that the red was blood,
And the door was half off its hinges, where
It was splintering, as I stood,
Then shapes began to appear to me,
Of soldiers, battering in
The Baltic Pine of this ancient door
To slay the soldiers within.

There wasn't a single sound to hear,
There should have been clash and roar,
A mighty battle was raging in
The Black Stone Tower of war.
I called and I called for Evelyn
But there wasn't a single trace
Of the love that I'd left alone in there,
That now, most terrible place.

I ran outside to the edge of the cliff
And stared down into the bay,
And there was the foulest, evil ship
Sails set, for sailing away.
And Evelyn strode down on the beach
While a soldier pulled at her hair,
Dragging her into a longboat as
She fought and struggled down there.

But this was a different Evelyn
To the one that I'd left at home,
The girl on the beach was dressed in peach,
My Evelyn dressed in bone,
And not in a full length courtly dress
Like you see from the days of yore,

As her ghostly shadow stepped in the boat
And sailed away from the shore.

I turned again to the Black Stone Tower
And the door was back in its frame,
There wasn't a sign of the bloody cross
That had been there, just as I came.
And Evelyn staggered from out the door
As I cried out, 'Where have you been?'
And she said sleepily, 'Don't be cross,
I've had an incredible dream!'

The Quest for Hieronymus Bosch

Hieronymus Bosch, who was only four,
Had toddled right out of my life,
I didn't know whether he'd gone on his own
Or left with the trouble and strife.
She'd rave and she'd threaten to fly the coop
As she said that my ways were strange,
But whether she'd bother to take him too
Would have meant a remarkable change.

'Why did you pick such a horrible name,'
She'd say, as she ladled the stew,
'You gave him the name of a painter insane,'
(As he baited the bears at the zoo).
'How can he live a commonplace life
With a moniker he can't spell?
You've sentenced your son to eternal strife
Like that panel, a painting of hell.'

Hieronymus, he didn't care about this,
He wanted to picture his world,
He'd flop and he'd slop in the mud, in his bliss,
And paint, till his toes had curled.
I knew that he'd be a surrealist when
He played with his mash, and was cute,
He swished it around on his palette to look
Like a man with a nose like a flute.

'That kid is so gruesome,' the wife had exclaimed,
'He's set on a roadway to hell.'
He'd crayoned a picture of me and her sister
Entwined on her favourite bell.
'He isn't like others,' I used to exclaim,
'He sees what he sees inside out,
He doesn't like others, like hair-splitting mothers,'
And that's when she started to shout.

I've searched and I've searched for Heironymus Bosch,
I'm trying to follow his trail,
The long line of beetles he captured in treacle,
The dead dog that's eating its tail.
I know that he's not with the trouble and strife
For she went into hiding in Greece,
He should be called Chester, the lad's such a jester,
I guess I'll be calling the Police.

Crystal Clear

She plaited her hair in a love-knot,
And stared at the crystal ball,
Sat in the gloom of a curtained room
At the end of a dim-lit hall,
And ghostly images floated in
Constrained by the curve of the glass,
She tried to reach, but beyond the breach
She could only sigh, alas.

His face was reflected from the light
That shone on the crystal ball,
He turned his eyes, not once but twice
To peer, as she tried to call,
For tears rolled desperately down her cheeks
As she stared at him, and cried,
'If only I'd stayed with you, my love,
If only I hadn't lied.'

But he'd caught the lie on her blushing cheek,
And he'd turned in pain away,
Oh, what she'd give to just relive
That scene on a summer's day,
The moment he knew her love was false
It ate away at his pride,
And what was reflected on his face
Now churned at her, inside.

Those present images in the ball
Gave way to a future spell,
And what was spawned from the present seed
Was reflected there, as well,

She saw him walk by a future love
Who was hid in her own doorway,
Who reached on out as he passed, to offer
Her lips, as he passed that way.

Then anger had her convulsed as he
Succumbed to that virgin kiss,
How could he turn to one so young
Had he had enough of this?
She seized a knife by the crystal ball
And thrust in the table top,
That future girl was a friend of hers
And she screamed at the image, 'Stop!'

She rushed on out to her friend who sat
Alone in the dim-lit hall,
'I've seen what you have planned, don't set
Your eye at my lover, Paul.
He's only gone for the moment now
But I know that he'll be back,
He's far too old for a girl like you,'
She had screamed in her attack.

'Well, listen now to the woman who
Is calling the kettle black,
You'll not be telling me what to do
For the loyalty you lack.
I'm well aware of the nights you spared
For another, now and then,
I have it straight from the horse's mouth
That you slept with my lover, Ben.'

The friends now stared at each other, in
A look that you'd call aghast,

There'd be no room for a friendship now
That the truth was out, at last.
And back in the gloom of a curtained room
In the unwatched crystal ball,
There stood the two in a different view
With blood, in the dim-lit hall.

She Loves Me Not...

He was one of the cognoscenti,
She was one of the 'up-for-sale',
I knew that I shouldn't fall for her
That she'd more than likely bale,
But she came to me as a short-stop
On the way to a better deal,
She wouldn't have even thought of,
(When she dumped me), how I'd feel.

I know it was my decision
To take her on at the start,
Then I didn't know the bad effect
She'd have upon my heart,
But she gave to me unstinting,
That was how she really was,
Right to the time the know-all came
And told her what was what.

She'd gaze in a fascination
As he'd run off at the mouth,
Telling us in his wisdom
What he'd learnt, both north and south.
I couldn't compete with his wallet,
I knew what his gifting cost,

And when he moved to the bedroom,
I knew that my cause was lost.

She shrugged it off in the morning,
She said it was only fair,
That I'd been suddenly just a friend
With benefits, to share,
But her life, it was slowly changing
And she sought stability,
That was the thing she found with him
That she couldn't find with me.

I saw them off to the movies,
I watched as they went to dine,
I saw him caress her everywhere
In places that were mine,
I thought that I couldn't stand it
The signs of their outward bliss,
Even though I had always known
In the end it would come to this.

But my love for her had curdled,
And my heart had turned to hate,
Revenge was upmost in my mind
When I planned an awful fate,
They ran around in a speedster,
A car with an open top,
I cut the lines to the power brakes
And I watched them both drive off.

I heard they were doing eighty
When the car didn't take the curve,
And smashed them into an old oak tree
As it leapt right over the curb,

They both were thrown clean over the hood,
He broke his neck on the tree,
And she was crippled below the waist
But he was dead, you see.

I'd visit her at the hospice
As her health returned to fair,
But nothing would change the fact that she
Would spend her life in a chair.
I'd push her out in the garden
As I felt repentance soar,
And she would cry, 'I want to die,'
While I fell for her, once more.

And she was happy to take me
At last, as the second best,
While in the guilt my tears were spilt
Though I tried to fake the rest,
I'm stuck with her in a wheelchair
And my life is merely dregs,
There isn't a single benefit
For a girl with crippled legs.

We can't make love in the morning,
We'll never dance at a ball,
I'm tied for life to a crippled wife,
It's my own fault, after all.
I shouldn't have given in to hate
For a love that wasn't mine,
And now I wonder if she loves me
Or just wants to pass the time.

Sin Binned

He'd only just raised the dustbin lid
When he saw the woman's head,
And what had impressed him most was that
It felt as heavy as lead,
It looked on up with its open eyes
With a stare that couldn't see,
Which made him fumble the lid and cry,
'It certainly wasn't me!'

He thought of the woman the head had been
Before they'd parted ways,
An older woman, but shorter now
Than he'd seen in former days,
He was on a nodding acquaintanceship
With the husband known as Jim,
And thought of him as a friendly bloke
But they'd still be hanging him.

He'd been on the rubbish round for years
So he knew most everyone,
But never a severed head before
Had been found on the rubbish run,
He hadn't an axe to grind with Jim
It was just Jim's lousy luck,
A man should allow for one mistake
So he tipped the head in the truck.

Then Jim came out and he waved at him
And he smiled, 'Good morning, Joe.'
While Joe smiled back, and he gave a grin
And said, 'How's the missis, Flo?'

'She's gone a little bit flighty, Joe,
Gone off for a spell,' he said,
'That tongue of hers, it was getting worse,
I'll swear she was off her head.'

'Well, ain't that just like a woman,' said
The man with the empty bin,
'I see you're light on your rubbish, are
There other bits to put in?'
'Plenty of time, I'll see to it
For the next time you come back,
I haven't had time to sort it out
But I'll bring it out in a sack.'

The following week he got two legs
And the feet were fairly strong,
And after he dumped them in the truck
He drove two doors along,
The bin outside held another head
Of a girl he knew as Tweet,
'It seems to be catching on, ' he thought,
As he drove along the street.

He didn't think to report it
It was no concern to him,
He only collected the rubbish that
They placed in a standard bin,
There wasn't a line in the regulations,
Not one that he'd read,
Of what to do when a bin was due
And it only held a head.

That street was becoming notorious
For the wives that went away,

Off for a spell to Dingley Dell
For a well earned holiday,
And Joe has quite a collection now
That lines his mantelpiece,
While Jane, his beau, says they've got to go,
Or she may well call the police.

The Shopfront Fire

The fire began in the cobbler's shop
In a terrace of shops that day,
And spread right through to the milliners
That was owned by Mrs. Gray,
It leapt up into the rooftop beams
And galloped along the street,
Burning a swathe through the fodder stores
And the blacksmith, Simon Fleet.

The smoke rose into an Autumn sky
And blackened the old clock tower,
It didn't pause, it was far too dry
For even an Autumn shower,
And Simon said, as the embers fell
To the household servant, Gert,
'The courtyard's starting to look like hell,
Get out of that silken skirt.'

He hadn't looked twice at Gert before
And she was so awful shy,
While he was never the greatest catch
With his horseshoe-looking eye,
But once he saw that the embers fell
He was more than kept alert,

He knew the fabric would burn like hell,
The silk in the servant's skirt.

She'd bought the skirt, it was second-hand
From a Drapers along the street,
It felt so silky and smooth, she'd said
From her waist down to her feet,
She liked the line of the skirt, the lads
Would see her pass, and stare,
So like the ladies she aped, she swore
To wear no underwear.

So Gert had blushed as she heard the words
Of the Blacksmith, Simon Fleet,
She wasn't going to show her legs
To Simon, out in the street,
The skirt went up with a sudden roar
And he heard her pitiful cries,
So trying his best to douse the flames
He wrapped canvas round her thighs.

The blaze was stopped by the corner shop
Where the fire engine stayed,
And kept from running its rampant course
Along the Grand Parade,
But Simon said it was Gertie's legs
That had failed her, in her pride,
But caught his eye with a tender sigh
As they fed the fire inside.

Whenever they speak of the shopfront fire
It's as if it paved the way,
The two have said, to the day they wed
And their happiness today,

For Gertie doesn't have charming looks
And he's ugly too, says Gert,
But Simon says it's a treat, that heat,
Under a silken skirt.

A Strange Courting

I never knew where she got the bones
But she spread them out in the grate,
And said to me that the way they fell
Would tell her about my fate.
I'd gone to her for the Tarot Cards,
I'd been told that she was a wiz,
But didn't know what a wizard was
Till I met this girl called Liz.

She wasn't a witch, she said to me,
For witches were too mundane,
They only had spells and love potions
And most of them were insane.
But she could look into the future with
The bones of the been and gone,
They helped to focus her visions on
The land of the to and from.

She spoke in riddles and teased my mind
In a language I didn't know,
I asked her what I was headed for,
She said I had far to go.
She told me about my love, Christine,
And the secret plans she bore,
She wasn't, as I had thought, pristine,
But had men in tow, by the score.

I asked her about the wedding that
We'd planned for along the track,
She said, I'd never be happy then,
Better get married in black.
She scattered the bones for a second time
And they fell about in the grate,
'If you go on with your plans,' she said,
'You're in for a dismal fate.'

'There's blood,' she said, 'and a kitchen knife,
A terrible slashing and cries,
'I don't know when, but it's after then,
And a crazy look in your eyes.
Then someone lies on the kitchen floor
In a horrible pool of blood,
And footprints there, and a tipped up chair
Where somebody walked in mud.'

The wedding went as we'd always planned,
I never gave it a thought,
And Christine put on my wedding band
She didn't think she'd be caught.
A man came round to the house one day
To say that Christine was his,
I took good note of his muddy boots
And suddenly thought of Liz.

He came at me with a kitchen knife
And said that he'd set her free,
I'd thought the knife had been meant for her,
But no, it was meant for me.
I seized his arm and we struggled then
While Christine stood in the door,

I somehow managed to turn the knife
And he lay dead on the floor.

'Why did you set him loose on me,'
I cried, 'the son of a gun,
What was the vow you made to me
That I'd be the only one.'
But Christine cried, and she knelt by him,
Her lover, down on the floor,
'I told him before he shouldn't come,
But he said that he loved me more.'

I was acquitted for self-defence
When the case came up for court,
And later I found that Christine went
She wasn't the loyal sort.
I went again to the Oracle
And I spilled the bones with Liz,
While she laid on me a gentle kiss
And said, 'It's what it is!'

Tale of an Ancient Sin

There was always an odour of sin around
The nave of that ancient church,
I knew of it as a choirboy,
I didn't have far to search,
The smell welled up in the vestry,
A sulphur and brimstone tang,
It leached on into our cassocks
When the bell for the matins rang.

The priest, he was old and doddering
And didn't look ripe for sin,
Old Father Coates may have sowed his oats
With nobody looking in,
But sin was there for a century,
It wasn't of recent time,
The stories told of a Father Golde
I heard from a friend of mine.

Back in the days when the church was strong
And it ruled the lives of all,
A Father Golde was the priest of old
And preached of the devil's fall,
When women came to confess their sins
And spoke of their evil deeds,
The priest took them at the altar there
In sin, and down on their knees.

The Nuns attached to the convent were
Obedient to his whim,
And many a cold and frosty night
He would call a sister in,
Her place, he said, was to warm his bed
To deter his chills, and ague,
And many a child was born in dread
To the parish, since the plague.

But one day after confessional
He had raped a Colonel's wife,
Who came to him with her petty sin
And described what it was like,
The priest, inflamed by her words and deeds
Had her pressed by the vestry door,
And who could know what she had to show
But the flagstones on the floor.

A troop of soldiers had marched on in
To assuage the Colonel's rage,
The moment the wife had gone back home
And told of the priest's outrage,
They seized the priest and they ran him through
With a sword right to the hilt,
Then tied him onto the cross outside
Where a sign outlined his guilt.

And every year on the first of June
You can hear the feet outside,
Marching up to the old church door,
The day that the father died.
A sense of sin that is coming in
As the church doors swing apart,
And blood appears on the altar in
The shape of an evil heart.

Near Thing!

The freighter loomed from the darkness
Its shadow high on our port,
And Jenny screamed at the starkness
Of the fate the freighter brought,
Its bow wave flowed right over the prow
Of our tiny little yacht,
We knew that we couldn't ride it out
So whether to swim, or not?

The sea was luckily clear and warm
It had been a perfect day,

As we had lazily sailed along
The length of Innotto Bay,
As night had fallen the breeze had too
And it left us quite becalmed,
So when the freighter came ploughing through
It had seen us both alarmed.

It rose above us, this rusty hulk
That had seen much better days,
The bridge was lit, could they see us sit
Where their bow cut through the waves?
The yacht was rocked by the turbulence
That its mighty hull displaced,
And suddenly we were swamped out there
As the sea rose to my waist.

The yacht had foundered, was going down
Crushed by the mighty bow,
And we fell into the sea where we
Clung on to each other, now.
It sucked us in as it glided past
And we heard the turgid roar,
As the giant props left a wake of froth
That would suck us in, for sure.

And Jenny panicked to stay afloat
As I clung on to her arm,
But down we went as our strength was spent
Where the props would do us harm,
We saw them thrash as we sank on down
And a dull throb filled our ears,
The blades would slice like a guillotine
Were the source of both our fears.

But the violent thrash of the water there
Sent currents beneath the stern,
And we were violently thrust on down
Where the props had ceased to churn,
And when we bobbed to the surface, we
Saw the freighter disappear,
Ploughing into the distance while
We lay in the bay, to cheer.

We were only a mile beyond the reef
And beyond that lay the land,
So struck out together in relief
And I held her by the hand,
We'll never forget that rusty hulk
As it passed, I caught it's name,
Riven with old corruption it
Was called, 'The Devil's Game!'

The Judgement

The Judge came into the village with
A troop of the finest horse,
The sunshine gleamed on their breastplates
And their guns and their swords, of course,
He wasn't there to be friendly, but
To make the rebels aware,
And carried the King's own warrant to
Set up his courthouse there.

The troop took over the Mason's Hall
The Judge took over the church,
And set up a bench down in the nave
As the troops set out to search,

They looked for the signs of weaponry
In the homes of the poorest men,
Tearing apart the hovels in
The search for the rebels, then.

To root out the roughshod army that
Had marched to defy the king,
Who tore up the standard prayer book
That the king was offering,
They forced the priests to reverse the mass
To the way it was done before,
Laying a siege to Exeter
In the way of a civil war.

Now the troops rode into the villages
And they held the men in chains,
Sworn to see that they paid in blood
For their temper, and their pains,
The women were wailing in the streets
As their men were taken in,
To answer to a black-hooded Judge
For their crimes against the King.

There wasn't a gallows large enough
For the men that he meant to hang,
But plenty of trees around the leas
That the cattle grazed upon,
And plenty of boughs and branches that
Would groan with the weight of men,
Whose only fault was this one revolt
When their faith was changed again.

They hung like fruit from the saplings,
They choked their lives from a limb,

They swung on ropes from the mighty oaks
In an orgy of suffering,
The farms lay waste in the country,
The crops lay waste in the fields,
There wasn't an army of labourers
Just troops, with their swords and shields.

The Judge climbed into his black teak coach
Rode out of the village grounds,
While children wailed and the women paled
In cutting their husbands down.
The horror lay in the children's genes
For generations, it's said,
Till years along they would right the wrong
By taking a bad king's head.

An Autumn Tale

The trees were talking in foreign tongues,
The leaves had plenty to say,
As he stood deep in the golden grove
Watching the treetops sway.
A gentle breeze had caught at their breath
To carry their whispered tales,
From tree to tree in the woodland depth
While the Autumn winds prevailed.

And golden leaves lay thick at their feet
A magic carpet of death,
Fluttering down with their lives complete
At the time of their final breath.
But she lay still on a mound of leaves
And smiled at the man she loved,

While he looked up like a man who grieves
At the sway of the trees above.

'Why is the Autumn fall so sad,
Could it be that they feel like us?
Their Summer went, and at last they're spent
And fall from the trees like dross.'
'They've had their season of love,' she sighed,
'While ours is still ahead,'
'But even we,' he had then replied,
'Face the day when we'll both be dead.'

He joined her down on the bed of leaves
And she kissed his lips and his brow,
'I never think about death,' she said,
'But only the here and now.'
'Don't you listen to what's been said,
Those fluttering leaves in the air,
They're asking, what's it like to be dead
In a tone of utter despair.'

'How could you know just what they say,
They're swaying trees in the breeze,
There isn't a dictionary, per se,
That a man can follow with ease.'
'Haven't you heard the tender moan
They make, when the wind soughs through,
Their sadness echoes in every tone
And it kills me, looking at you.'

'You have to stop, you're frightening me,'
She said as she pulled away,
'I thought that we came to make sweet love
On a beautful Autumn day.'

'But what will we think when our skin is dry,
And wrinkled, so many years,
Maybe the love that we feel today
Will lie in a horse-drawn hearse.'

He looked again and he watched her age
So brittle, an Autumn leaf,
Dry and brown, he was looking down
While she stared with eyes of grief.
'You've taken away our springtime, Joe,
And reached for the Autumn rain,
I only know that I have to go
And I'll not come here again!'

Of Loss and Love

He hadn't been home a day before
He found that his wife had died,
The doctor said it was sudden, that
There was something wrong inside.
He couldn't be more specific till
The autopsy was done,
He'd have to wait for a week for that,
'It's the same for everyone.'

He went on back to an empty home
And then he gave way to grief,
It wasn't as if he had a friend
To offer him some relief,
He'd been away on the ocean swell
On a Tramp from Amsterdam,
For six months out of eleven when
He should have been home, with Pam.

A sailor's life is a lonely life
He had known that from the start,
He possibly shouldn't have taken a wife
When they'd be so far apart,
For seven years they had worked it out
And his wife had said she'd cope,
But loneliness is a dreadful thing
When you're living your life in hope.

He'd loved her well and she loved him too
In their sentimental way,
She'd managed to hide her tears each time
That his ship had sailed away,
But once he had seen the autopsy
It had torn him quite apart.
It seems his wife had despaired of dreams
And died of a broken heart.

He didn't go back to sea at once
But he hung around in bars
And managed to get himself so drunk
That all he could see was stars,
He thought his grief would diminish as
The days had turned into years,
But love for him didn't finish, it
Just seemed to work in reverse.

He even took down her pictures, and
He locked them all in a drawer,
He didn't want the reminder of
What he had lost before,
But life is a game of chances and
It never will be denied,

He met a nurse when he found her purse
And something lit up inside.

It seemed her job was a lot like his
She was always working shifts,
They met whenever they could, and he
Found he was buying gifts,
He went away on a Tramp again
But just one month at a time,
And she was waiting when he returned
Like a welcome carafe of wine.

He spent some time at the cemetery
To honour his wife, his Pam,
And she asked if she could come along
To which he had said, 'You can.'
He wed the girl in the early Spring
And he found a job ashore,
And swore he'd never go back to sea,
She couldn't have loved him more.

The Final Solution

He was walking along the tramway
On the other side of town,
The lines had shone in the darkness,
There wasn't a tram around,
The road from the rain was glistening
Reflecting the roadside lights,
Then the man stood still, and listening
On this coldest of winter nights.

It had been so still and silent
Once the shoppers all had fled,
Out of the city centre,
And heading on home to bed,
But he was one of the homeless
Adrift on the city's streets,
And prey to the wind and weather
That the homeless people meet.

His coat was ragged and weathered,
His boots were holed in the soles,
He hadn't managed a shave for days
So his beard looked grey and old,
His pants, held up by a piece of string
Were the sorriest in the town,
And his face was racked with misery,
For he looked just beaten down.

But now as the lights of the bedrooms died
On either side of the street,
The dark was becoming palpable
As he dragged his weary feet,
But still he stuck to the tramway lines
As the quickest way to the docks,
Hoping to find a brazier's heat
To dry out his sodden socks.

But still he stood and he listened
For sounds in that dreadful night,
It seemed that animals snapped and snarled
Beyond the reach of light,
The homeless went with a rumour
There were wolves out there in the dark,
For many a trace of blood was found
By day, out there in the park.

And there in the dark of alleyways
He could see the eyes a-gleam,
Waiting for him to pass them by
Before they would pounce, it seemed,
He shivered under his ragged coat
And pulled the collar up high,
Thinking it might protect his throat
When they came for him, by and by.

The wolves then bayed at the crescent moon
As they watched his figure pass,
They saw him shaking in fear and gloom
Like walking on broken glass,
But suddenly there was a rumbling
And the lights of a late night tram,
He moved aside then as if to ride
When a wolf tore at his hand.

Then suddenly there were three or four
In a fury of rip and snarl,
Tearing apart a bag of bones
Of the man who was known as Carl,
His blood seeped into the tramway tracks
As the tramway driver stopped,
And watched as they tore the man apart
With one of the city cops.

The council workers came out at dawn
To clear up the grisly mess,
They'd had their orders from City Hall
To dispose of homelessness,
The keepers, out from the city zoo
Recaptured the wolves out there,

But ready to let them out again
When a killing was in the air.

'We have to clean up the city streets,'
The mayor had long opined,
'Get rid of the homeless, nice and neat,
The residents sure won't mind.'
The street's a virtual jungle when
The lights in the streets go out,
And all you'll hear is the scream of fear
When a homeless person shouts.

The Battle on the Footplate

They'd never got on before the dance
And they certainly wouldn't now,
For Geoffrey Raise had showered praise
On the Fireman's girl, somehow,
And she, Charlene, was impressed, it seems
With the Engine driver's call,
And changed her date, though it seemed too late
To the Fireman, at the ball.

They stood on the plate of the Duke of Kent
With the fireman raising steam,
Shovelling coal to the firebox
In a movement swift and clean,
He scattered the coals on the glowing bed
With a practised twist of his wrist,
While the driver kept his eyes ahead
As the steam built up, and hissed.

'Why did you jump on Charlene then,'
Said the Fireman, Henry Rice,
During a break, his back was bent
With sweat, but his eyes were ice,
'I don't have to answer to you,' said Raise,
'Charlene was anyone's girl,
I liked the way that she held herself
And she sure knew how to twirl.'

The train pulled out of the station with
A puff and a cloud of steam,
And clattered along the track from Klifft
On its way to Essingdean,
Pulling a dozen coaches and
A Guards van at the rear,
And a hundred and twenty passengers
At the high time of the year.

'What would you say if I did to you
What you did to me, back then,
Cutting in on your date that night,
What was her name, that Gwen?'
'She wouldn't have looked at you,' said Raise,
As he pulled the chord to toot,
'And as far as your feelings go, old chum,
I really don't give a hoot.'

The train was rocketing down the line,
And flew past the water tower,
While Raise had opened the cocks right up
To give the Express more power,
The gauge was inching at sixty five
As they flew past Barton Dale,
While Rice was shovelling coal once more
Though his face was pinched and pale.

He took Raise down with the shovel as
They raced through Weston Town,
Who lay, half stunned on the footplate
Hanging off and looking down.
He kicked on out at the Fireman with
His size twelve steel-capped boots,
Who reached and hung on the chord that gave
The Duke of Kent its toots.

The train was racking up seventy five
As they kicked and punched and swore
Totally out of control it passed
The Halt at Elsinore,
They narrowly missed a rumbling freight
As the points took it aside,
While Raise had yelled, 'You can go to hell,
But control your wounded pride.'

The Fireman opened the firebox
Spraying hot coals on the plate,
'Now dance again as you danced Charlene,
If you think that you're oh so great.'
'Just let me get to my feet,' said Raise
'Or you're going to wreck the train.'
'It might be time,' said the Fireman,
'For your life to fill with pain.'

They hit the buffers at Essingdean
And the engine left the track,
It leapt up over the platform as
The roof ripped off the stack.
Raise was told when they went to court
That he'd never be re-hired,

And Rice, for want of the girl he sought,
The Fireman was fired.

After Dark

A panic would settle all over her face
Each night as she pulled the blinds,
'The world outside is a scarier place
Whenever the day unwinds.
I've seen the changes that darkness brings
When the lights in the street go out,
There are screams and cries, and animal things,
Can you say what it's all about?'

I said I couldn't, it wasn't the same
For me as it was for her,
'The night is merely a lack of light
But nothing has changed out there.
The lamposts stand, they may not be lit
But they're still upright in the dark,
And as for sounds, and animal things
These are merely dogs in the park.'

'Dogs don't howl, or bay at the moon,
They don't have a Lion's roar,
And what sits tearing, out in the gloom
Just out from our own front door?
A line of vultures sit on our fence,
Flapping their wings for prey,
While howls and grunts are making me tense
The moment the day's away.'

'I'll take you out and I'll prove you're wrong,
There's nothing to fear outside,
It may be dark but the world goes on
There's just a turn in the tide.'
'I wouldn't dare, there's a sickly moon
That beams on down from a height,
It has a sheen, and the sheen is green
Whenever I put out the light.'

'And who is the man at night who roams
Out there on the cobblestones,
You said it's the window cleaner man
But the window cleaner's Jones.
And Jones is tucked in his tiny bed
By the time the clock strikes nine,
I know it's true, for his wife has said,
And his wife's a friend of mine.'

'It's only some ragged, passing tramp
Or a gypsy, out for the air,
They park their vans on the common land
Where the village holds its fair.'
'He jingles coins as he walks on by,
And hums, but it's out of tune,
You'd see, if ever you part the blinds
Him walking under the moon.'

I'd had enough, and opened the door,
And took her out to the porch,
I felt so confident I was right
I didn't carry a torch.
We walked a way out into the street
She shivered and gripped my arm,
I waved my hand in a calming sweep,
'You see? No cause for alarm.'

The air was suddenly filled with bats,
And some were caught in her hair,
While round our feet, a scurry of rats
Brought screams to the street out there.
The vultures sat there flapping their wings,
And launched themselves from our fence,
A man was jingling coins, walked past
Then I knew why my wife was tense.

I dragged her back through the open door,
All bleeding and cut and hurt,
Pulled the bats from her tangled hair
And the ones attached to her skirt,
We never venture outside at night
Not after we pull the blinds,
But leave the world of the after dark
To the man who jingles the coins.

The Yellow Bag

They'd arranged to meet on Charter Street
At the point that midnight chimed,
She was to come with a yellow bag,
And he with a book of rhyme,
The ad had run in the Daily Mail
And had said, and here I quote:
'Wanted: A gentleman for fun
With a high speed motor boat.'

Then he'd replied that he had the boat
Could she bring along the fun,

And she wrote back, 'Nice to meet you, Jack,
I have fun for everyone.'
He saw her in front of the Gaumont
That had played 'The Cruel Sea',
Standing there with a yellow bag
And thought, 'That's the one for me!'

He wandered up and he waved the book
With the title 'Nonsense Rhyme',
She gave him a cool, appraising look
Like a laid back Valentine.
'It's much too late for the boating lake,'
He said, 'Would you like a drink?'
And she stood there with a vacant stare
But replied, 'What do you think?'

He led her down to the Castle Club
Where he had a private booth,
Then sat her down till the drinks came round
And remarked upon her youth.
She raised a brow when he asked her how
She had come to advertise,
She said, 'It's something I have to do
If I need to meet new guys.'

They drank their drinks and they talked a bit
About nothing much, per se,
And then he asked her about the fun
But she said he'd have to pay.
'I thought a ride in my motor boat
Would be payment,' he began,
To which she said, 'I'm not free to ride,
I'm a working courtesan.'

While back in the heart of Charter Street
Where the leaves blew from the trees,
A girl stood there in a party dress
And the wind blew round her knees,
She'd been in watching 'The Cruel Sea'
For the time had seemed to lag,
But now stood out on an empty street
Holding her yellow bag.

The Devil Park

She said, 'Let's go to the Devil Park,'
At noon, on a summer's day,
I said, 'We'd better go after dark,
They hide themselves away.
They only come out to feed at night
So that's when you see them best,
By day, they never come out to play,
That's when they get to rest.'

We packed the car and we took a torch,
A powerful, bright spotlight,
The only way we would see them there
On a dark and gloomy night,
We waited till it was just on dusk
Then finally hit the road,
The Park was seventy miles away
Or an hour, I'd been told.

The gate of the park was locked and barred
But we scaled and climbed across,
That's when Giselle had torn her dress,
It was old, so no great loss,

We could hear the scrabbling and the screech
Of the small marsupials,
Grubbing around the park for food
And giving out grunts and squeals.

The torch lit up in a long wide arc
As we scanned across the ground,
The first one that we saw had roared
When it knew it had been found,
Its jaw was wide and its evil teeth
Could give you a nasty bite,
I wasn't going to get too close
On that warm and sultry night.

We'd wandered round for an hour out there
Had seen groups of two's and three's,
And some that were more adventurous
We could see were climbing trees,
When out of the darkness came a voice
That was grating, cold and hard,
'What do you think, by coming here
To spy in my own backyard?'

It made me start, for the torch wheeled round
To illuminate a stump,
And there a figure in shiny black
Was sat, and it made us jump,
The face was narrow and pointed, leered,
Was capped with a pair of horns,
While a long black tail with snake-like scales
Flicked up, like it meant to warn.

'We came to see the marsupials,'
I stuttered, in my distress,

'We meant no harm, but you just alarmed
Us both, in your fancy dress.'
'You broke in here, but I see the fear
That I cause you, out in the dark,
What did you think you'd find out here,
You've come to the Devil's Park.'

The Devil slowly uncurled himself
And he stood up, ten feet tall,
I saw his claws and his evil jaws
And his goat-like legs, and all,
'You both may need to redeem yourselves
By paying your court to me,
I'll make you the lord and lady of
All of the land you see.'

And suddenly all the park was lit
In a ghostly, evil glow,
He said, 'I can give you all of it,
I have the power, you know.'
'I think that you've tried that line before,'
I said, in a sudden shot,
'And "get thee behind me Satan" was
The answer that you got.'

A flame curled out of the Devil's mouth
As he opened up his jaw,
And fixed me with a piercing glare
As he beat his chest, to roar,
'You'll not escape, for I'll cast my cape
To capture your sinful souls,
And when we meet, it will be a treat
In your seat of glowing coals.'

He threw his cape in a whirl until
It covered him like a shroud,
And then went up in a puff of smoke,
As Giselle cried out, aloud,
We raced on back and we scaled the gate
In a massive leap in the dark,
I said, 'Don't ever suggest again
We visit the Devil Park!'

A Fateful Blow

The clattering wind came back again
In the cold, dark hours of the morn,
There must have been such a mighty wind
In the hour that I was born.
For I went outside to savour it,
I love the wind in the trees,
Anything from a sultry blow
To an ice cold winter breeze.

And Miriam always chided me
I should keep the door pulled to,
'You may delight in the wind at night
I don't share in that with you.'
'Doesn't it tell you the earth's alive
When it's breathing, Oh so hard?'
'That may be so, but just keep the blow
Trapped in our own backyard.'

It rattles around the chimney pots,
It lifts the tin on the roof,
And drives the rain to the window pane
As if to say, 'Here's proof!'

Proof that the world's alive and well
When it howls and plucks at the eaves,
And swaying each branch so you can tell
By filling the air with leaves.
'I don't see the purpose that it serves,'
Miriam used to shout,
The wind replied and she almost died
When it blew the hearth fire out.
Hurtling down the chimney flue
Like a gale she'd made inside,
I said, 'Just watch what you say and do,
Even the wind has pride!'

I'd say that the two were enemies
From the time she opened her mouth,
'It's wrecking my pink anemones
When it blows from the freezing south.'
I told her to hold her anger in,
She was weak, the wind was strong,
She hadn't the power to save her bower
While it knew not right from wrong.

It came to a head when she slammed the door
On an innocent springtime breeze,
And sealed her fate when she muttered hate,
She was brought down to her knees.
Walking along the clifftop path
As she did, and both of us must,
A sudden blow sent her over, though
It was merely a random gust.

I go each week to the cemetery
And I leave anemones,
While lurking around the headstones there
Is her ancient enemy,

If only she'd kept her tongue in check
She would still be here with me,
Not lying beneath a howling gale
In the local cemetery.

The Stepfather

Since ever he came to live at our house
We'd never felt safe or sure,
So late at night we'd turn out the light
And block up the bedroom door,
We'd slide a heavy old chest in place
That he never could push right in,
We knew, with just one look at his face,
The man was riddled with sin.

Our mother, bless her, was long divorced,
Our father was gone for good,
He never called, and we were appalled
That he never came when he should.
'Why do you need that man in the house,'
I said, 'You have me and Drew.'
But she would smile, 'Well, it's been a while,
And there's things that you can't do.'

We didn't know what she meant back then
For we were too young to know,
How a woman's won, or she bears a son,
Where a man and a woman go.
We only knew he was far too nice
When he first came into our home,
His creepy fingers, they felt like ice
So we wished he'd leave us alone.

He'd wander about the house by night,
We'd hear him mounting the stair,
And feigning sleep, not let out a peep
When we heard him breathe out there.
He'd come to a halt by our bedroom door
And stand and listen, we thought,
The tears in my brother's eyes would glisten
In fear that we'd be caught.

His frightful stare gave a mighty scare
When he fixed on Drew and I,
Our mother said it was really sad
That he had just one good eye.
His other eye, it was made of glass
He had lost that one in the war,
It never closed, so we both supposed
That he slept, but still he saw.

Our house lay at the top of a hill
And a milk cart stood outside,
Its great cartwheels were covered in steel
And to hold it, it was tied.
One day we loosened the holding chain
As he came out into the street,
And watched the cart as it rolled on down,
Knocking him off his feet.

A wheel rolled slowly over his head
As he gave a deathly sigh,
His brains on the road were grey and red
And the pressure popped his eye.
It lay and stared at the two of us,
Was accusing us then, and still,

The memory sits and stays with us
For we'd never meant to kill.

Our mother wailed, and our mother mourned
And she kept his one glass eye,
She propped it up on the mantelpiece
'So he's with us still,' she'd sigh.
Drew would shudder and I would shake
As it followed us round the room,
We both grew up with a complex that
We'll never get over soon.

Like Mother...

When I met, and married my wife,
I opened a secret door,
I knew that her mother, Grace, was strange
But I didn't know what for.
They spoke so low that I couldn't hear
In a mother/daughter pact,
But Ellen, she was my holy grail
Til I found it was an act.

I'd been brought up in the English way
Of roast beef, fruit and veg,
The mint that grew and the rhubarb too
By our garden's privet hedge,
I didn't know there were other things
That were quite beyond my ken,
But she'd come up through a different school
Though I didn't know it then.

They say you should check the mother out
If you want to save your tears,
For what the mother is like right now
Is your wife in thirty years,
And Grace was skinny and pastie-faced
With a rock-hard, gimlet eye,
While Ellen was soft and curvy then
And just a trifle shy.

Grace was running a cuisine club
For the village ladies all,
Every Wednesday they'd go *en masse*
Down to the village hall,
Ellen said there were treats in store
But I didn't really see,
Not til she brought it home with her
That she'd try it out on me.

The first of the treats she brought on home
Almost knocked me through a loop,
I said, 'What's that in the steaming bowl,'
And she answered 'Batwing soup.
You might need a knife and fork for it,
The wings have a leathery feel,
It won't take long to get used to it
It tastes a little like eel.'

After I'd gagged and choked a bit
I managed to keep some down,
I said, 'I'd rather have beef, my love,'
But she stood awhile, and frowned,
'I've made you a special omelette,
Of turtle legs and bees,
Bound together by turkey eggs
And just a little cheese.'

I couldn't say what I thought of it,
She would be dismayed, my wife,
I knew the love she'd put into it
It would only cause us strife,
But every Wednesday she'd bring one home
A treat for me to try,
Her casserole was a lucky dip
And snake in her cottage pie.

I suffered it for a month or more
Then I put my case to her,
'I draw the line at toadskin wine,
And a pie with rodent fur,
I love you, Ellen, I really do
But your mother gives me the creeps,
Her witches recipes just won't do,
I hate ragwort and leeks.'

We came to a final arrangement,
She could do what she'd always done,
The whisk broom under the stairs, she said
Was her idea of fun,
I try to ignore the pointy hat
That she wears when the moon is high,
But she never feeds me toads and rats
Though her mother asks her, 'Why?'

The Gathering In...

The carts rolled out of the warehouses
And trawled each single street,
Each drawn by a giant Clydesdale with
Those massive hooves and feet,
They creaked along, and they struck a gong
That excited furtive looks,
While the men that day, who rode the dray
Called out, 'Bring out your books.'

They watched the shimmer of curtains as
The people peeked outside,
For many were loth to show themselves,
All they had left was pride,
The law brought in by the looney left
Trapped all but the pastrycooks,
For they could retain their recipes
At the cry, 'Bring out your books.'

They said they were saving forests from
The pulp mill on the bay,
There wouldn't need to be paper with
The pads we have today,
And too many things were incorrect
Had been printed on a tree,
Were sitting on people's shelves, defunct
In ideology.

The people set up resistance, they
Had loved their tattered tomes,
And many a shelf was burdened in
The meanest of their homes,

'The government's trying to dumb us down,'
Was the universal cry,
'Go out and save the forests, but
If they're already printed, why?'

The spread of ideas is dangerous
They could rot you to the core,
And too many things on liberty
Have been printed, long before,
Perhaps it would have been better if
The people couldn't read,
Taking away the books at last
Might take away the need.

The drays that rumbled along each street
They had stacked the books up high,
But there was the odd revisionist
Who complained, and grumbled, 'Why?'
A squad broke into each suspect house
Where the owner locked the door,
And tore the books from his fevered grasp
While screaming, 'It's the law!'

But mine, I hid in the garden shed
And buried the others deep,
They wouldn't be getting their hands on them
The ones that I wished to keep,
There's so many fake and useless things
That they're legislating for,
But to take our books and our liberty
Would be like declaring war.

The Harkness Light

We lived on a tiny spit of land
That they called the Harkness Light,
It sat on a reef, a mile of sand
And it beamed out through the night,
There was just myself, and my darling wife
By the name of Jennifer,
But when I went up to tend the light,
He was below, with her.

I was supposed to be on my own
But he brought the cutter out,
Every time that they feared a storm
He'd come, and put her about,
Tie her up to the wooden dock
When the tide was on the rise,
And burst on in to our tiny room
With a wild look in his eyes.

'I've come to be of assistance, Joe,
There's a storm front coming in,'
'I think we can manage it ourselves,'
I'd say, with a touch of vim,
I never could trust those smiling eyes
Or that set of perfect teeth,
He made me think of a circling shark
Like the ones beyond the reef.

But Jennifer always welcomed him
With one of her gracious smiles,
She hadn't a frown for anyone
And her smile would beam for miles,

'It's lovely to have some company,'
She'd say, when a storm was nigh,
And cold, black angry thunderheads
Had filled the darkening sky.

He wasn't of any assistance, he
Would sit and drink our tea,
While I would climb to the light alone
He wasn't much use to me,
I began to suspect his visits there
Were more to do with her,
I knew that he was attracted to
My darling Jennifer.

It came to a head one night when I
Came down to find them hushed,
With Jennifer disarranged, and when
I looked at her, she blushed,
I knew that I had to do something
But what? It chilled my blood,
That one of these days she'd slip away
And I'd lose my wife for good.

I said, 'I need your assistance, Chris,
To change the carbon arc,
We'd better get up on top or else
All they will see is dark.
I followed him up the winding stair
But carried a bar of lead,
And when we arrived at the topmost stair
I hit him, over the head.

It doesn't take much to truss a man
When he's out, stone cold for the count,

I tied his back to the outer rail
And facing the light, its mount,
And then I plastered his eyelids wide
So he couldn't take his sight
Away from that glaring carbon arc
That made up the Harkness Light.

'What do you think you're doing?' Chris
Had screamed on his coming to,
I said, 'I'm protecting Jennifer
From the leery eyes of you.
You shouldn't come on to another's wife
For you know, it's just not right,
I'll do whatever I have to do
If it makes you see the light.'

That light burnt into his very brain
As he cursed, and cried, and swore,
His eyes could never survive the pain
Of a million candle power,
I went below and I said to her
'Go up and set him free,
You'll have to gentle him down the stair,
I don't think he can see.'

It seems that I bet on a loser
For she left me anyway,
'How could you be so cruel,' she said,
As she left, the following day,
I heard they're living together now
But I'm comforted at night,
That when she strips off her clothes for him
All he sees is the Harkness Light.

The Shadow Makers

He only appears in the pouring rain
When all the gutters are clogged,
I asked if anyone knew his name
They said, but my ears were blocked.
There wasn't a thing you could hear out there
For the water, bubbling through,
The rain's refrain in a noisy drain,
The thunder and lightning too.

You'd see his shadow on distant walls
Thrown there by a gaslight flare,
And catch the shape of his stovepipe hat
Flitting both here and there,
They say he's waiting for dollymops
Just as they're starting to run,
As night is chasing the day away
And rain's blotting out the sun.

Then rumour has it, the Ripper's back
We're waiting for blood and gore,
We're tense, awaiting the first attack,
For that's what the Ripper's for.
They say he chews on his victim's bones
Then eats their liver and all,
The streets will fill with their awful groans
As blood will spatter a wall.

And then the sound of a horses hooves
Pulling a Landau coach,
Its wheels a-rattle on cobblestones
Just as he cuts their throats,

Perhaps he'll lure them to take a ride
In that black, square box on wheels,
Then all that slashing goes on inside,
God knows how a razor feels.

We sit and muse in the Hemlock Inn
A dollymop on our laps,
And feed the terror they feel within
Filling in most of the gaps.
They turn to us for protection then
So we gain their favours cheap,
And keep on telling those same old tales
Til the bawds curl up, and weep.

Whenever the fog and the mist are thick
And the lamplight's just a glow,
We make our way to the Hemlock Inn
Where the skirts are raised, you know,
Then say his shadow's been seen again
Just to make the bawds all shriek,
'He's getting ready to pounce, and then...'
He'll be there again, next week.

Index of First Lines